Matty and the
Moonlight Horse

Matty and the Moonlight Horse

by Jane Ayres

Copyright: Text© 2005 Jane Ayres
Published by Pony, Stabenfeldt A/S
Cover illustration: Jennifer Bell
Cover layout: Stabenfeldt AS

Typeset by Roberta Melzl
Edited by Bobbie Chase
Printed in Germany 2005

ISBN: 1-933343-06-0

Stabenfeldt, Inc.
457 North Main Street
Danbury, CT 06811
www.pony.us

Chapter 1

I want to tell you all about my favorite horses and ponies. I have three – no, four – no; well, let's face it, I love them all. Soames is a great big cobby bay with long ears and dinner plate feet, and he loves people but hates other ponies. He gets jealous when they come near him and lays back his long ears and kicks. But he's great to ride; full of enthusiasm and energy, and he jumps like a cat.

Then there's Bessie, who's stocky and black, and very moody. If she's in one of her funny moods, and you happen to be riding her on the lunge rein, she suddenly breaks into a canter and gets faster and faster until you become dizzy and feel as if you're on one of those mechanical merry-go-round ponies. But if she's in a good mood, she nuzzles your hair and dribbles on your face and you forget how naughty she can be.

Then there's Elliott, a zippy little skewbald with a sticky-up white mane and wire brush tail and the bumpiest trot you could ever imagine, and Busker, the elderly Exmoor mare who is blind in one eye, and Everest, the silver-gray retired show pony who won over five hundred rosettes, and Penny … I could go on and on, I suppose.

You're probably thinking, lucky thing, how come she's got all these ponies? She must have wealthy parents or live on a stud farm or something. Well, to tell you the truth, they're not actually my ponies.

I don't live in a large, expensive house or a wonderful farm in the country. I live in a modest house on a busy street with nice parents who aren't rich at all. My best friend Ronnie (it's actually Veronica, but she would kill me if I told you that) lives next door. And my name is Matty. Matty Mathews. That's what my friends call me. (My real name is Octavia. Can you believe it? What were my parents thinking? Why do parents do that to their kids?)

Anyway, I'm thirteen and a half, of medium height and build, with blue eyes and short mousey brown hair – no distinguishing features to speak of. I blend into the crowd, Ronnie tells me, although I have yet to discover whether this is a virtue or not. She, on the other hand, is strikingly pretty with emerald green eyes and a mass of copper-gold hair that she wears in a French braid, very chic.

My favorite ponies actually belong to our local riding school, which is run by an odd middle-aged woman named Miss Pugh. There are ten ponies and two horses, and the stables are kind of squashed between a burger joint and a used car lot, at the back of an old housing development. This means that you always have to ride down the main road and cross two busy streets before reaching the field where most of the lessons are held.

To be honest, it's not a very good riding school and Miss Pugh is a terrible teacher. I don't really think she knows that much about ponies, and in fact the riding school used to belong to her brother, who was an ex-army major and *did* know something. But when he moved to Australia she carried on anyway, although really it's her two head girls who keep the place going and run most of the lessons. I think the owner of the car lot has offered to buy her out so he can expand his business, but for some reason she has never accepted. I don't know why. She never touches the ponies if she can help it, and she always wears a pink or turquoise suit at the stables, with great jangly bracelets that frighten the ponies, bright orange lipstick, and too much powder. (And Ronnie says that fire-red can't possibly be her natural hair color).

Despite all this, Ronnie and I spend every free minute at the stables because, as you will have gathered, we love being near the ponies. Mom calls us ponymad and says we're obsessed, but that one day we'll grow out of it and be like normal teenagers. She's wrong, of course. By the time I'm as old as Mom I plan to live on a huge farm with lots of land and at least thirty horses, and I will probably be a famous show jumper or dressage rider, and when Mom comes over to visit I'll say to her, "See, Mom? I didn't grow out of it, I kept growing into it." I'd like to see what she has to say then.

In the meantime, I, like Ronnie, and my other friends Spike and Gina, hang around at Miss Pugh's stables working for rides. I have to say, though, that we seem to have to do a lot of mucking out, scrubbing buckets and cleaning tack before a free ride is offered.

"I wonder how many other kids your age get exploited like this?" Dad comments from time to time over supper, but he doesn't understand. Of course, if you are as pony-mad as I am, I know that you will understand. In fact, you are probably saying to yourself, "So, she spends all her time at the stables, working for rides. She and a million other girls. So what? What makes her different?" And you might just be getting a little bit irritated because you are expecting some kind of story, an adventure perhaps, and so far you've just heard me babbling on about my favorite ponies. Be patient.

It's 7:15 on a warm and balmy July morning. My alarm clock is beeping furiously. (It's on the other side of the room to make sure that I have to get out bed to switch if off). I groan, scowl at the clock, and then, remembering it's Saturday, ignore it for one more precious minute before rolling ungraciously out of bed. I land on last night's upturned soda mug, the remaining dregs staining the baggy tee-shirt I wear in bed. I stand up, curse, and trip over the jodhpur boots I left in the middle of the floor with dirty jeans and assorted underwear.

I am not a morning person.

At 7:30 I head downstairs. I hover in the kitchen doorway, mumble incoherently at my mother, who doesn't look up from the women's magazine she is reading at the table, and slump beside her onto one of our hard wooden chairs.

"Orange juice's in the jug," she says.

I nod and pour myself a glass.

"I wish you wouldn't wear those filthy jeans," she remarks in the resigned voice that I know so well. "People will think we don't wash our clothes in this household. They'll think you're a neglected child."

"I couldn't find a clean pair," I reply, becoming slowly revived by the sugar.

"I'm not surprised, the state your room is in."

I grunt.

We sit in silence for a while and I mentally go over my plan for the day. I have a routine for Saturdays. Get up. Eat breakfast. Get moaned at by Mom. Meet Ronnie. (She will knock on the door any minute now). Walk to the stables. (This will take about ten minutes unless we stop at the drug store for chocolate supplies). Meet Gina and Spike. Commiserate on our pony-less state. Moan about Miss Pugh. Muck out all the stalls.

10

Sweep the yard. Wash the water buckets. Groom the ponies. Sympathize with Gina for getting slobbered on by Bessie (again). Pray that someone cancels a lesson so one of us gets a free ride. Try not to get too miffed if only one of us gets a free ride. Clean tack. Eat our sandwiches. Sweep yard again. Etc.

Change in today's routine – we are all going swimming in the town's outdoor pool at 4:30.

"I suppose you're off to that run-down old riding school again," remarks Dad emerging from the back garden, armed with pruning shears.

I almost say, "No, why would I be, with my riding boots and helmet? I'm just off to do some shopping." I'm still trying to think of a witty comeback when the back door opens and Ronnie pokes her head in, smiling radiantly.

"Good morning, Mrs. Mathews. Mr. Mathews. Nice day, isn't it?"

My parents smile back and return the greeting, and I can see that what's going through their minds is, "Why isn't *our* daughter as pleasant and charming?"

"Ready, Matty?" chirps Ronnie. I grab my lunch-box and follow her outside, wondering why her teeth are neat and straight and mine aren't.

Ronnie and I have been best friends since we were six years old, when her parents first moved next door. Unlike me, an only child, Ronnie has two younger brothers, Douglas and Kirk, identical twins, currently three years old and both attending nursery school, thank goodness. They are noisy and boisterous and quite often drive us both crazy. Ronnie's Mom gave up her job as an assistant librarian to look after them, although she says that when they're old enough she'll go back to work. My Mom and Ronnie's Mom both go to the same aerobics class on Monday nights and are good friends, which I think is really nice. And both of our fathers play in the same local amateur jazz band (Dad plays clarinet and Ronnie's Dad is a drummer) and seem to get along well.

It makes life so much easier when best friends' families get along. Not like poor Gina and Spike. Gina's Mom is stuck-up and neurotic and would prefer it if Gina were the same. She does not approve *at all* of Spike, who she says is weird because she once shaved off all her hair (it's growing back now) and wears six earrings in each ear, and both of her parents are always protesting on behalf of environmental causes, and they actually were arrested once. If she gave them a chance she would see that Spike's parents are great people, kind and generous, both with very respectable jobs as computer programmers, and probably earning lots more money than any of ours. And Spike, despite appearances, is the brainiest girl in the class and will probably become a famous scientist. Anyway, Gina's Mom (her Dad left home years ago) forbade Gina ever to see Spike again, so Gina has to see her in secret and lie to her Mom, which she hates doing, and we all try to cover for her. Honestly, what parents can drive you to!

We walk into the stable yard and see Spike leading a tiny toddler for a lunge lesson on Busker, Miss Pugh attacking a cup of coffee before beginning the lesson, and Gina filling a water bucket. And through it all, my eyes fix on a vision of loveliness. Standing outside a stall, dish face held high, neat ears alert, snow-white coat gleaming in the sun, is a beautiful Welsh mare. She gazes into my eyes. I gaze back.

"She doesn't look like the usual sort of pony that Miss Pugh buys," remarks Ronnie, recovering her powers of speech quicker than I.

"Girls, would one of you tack up the new pony for the 9:30 lesson?" shouts Miss Pugh. "Spike, make sure you have the lunge rein for Busker. Come along, then."

She grabs a lunge whip and sets off purposefully. Spike pulls a face behind her back but follows with Busker and the toddler.

"See you later."

While Ronnie, Gina and I muck out the stables and tidy the yard, we discover from one of the older girls that the new horse, *Snowstorm*, arrived at the stables the previous evening, and that she is a Welsh section B mare, eight years old and from a very good stud farm.

By now, several students are arriving and someone tries to organize a mini procession down to the field for the lesson. Gina disappears into Elliott's box armed with a body brush and comb and I guess that she is going for another fruitless attempt at making his brillo-pad mane lie flat. Perhaps Gina is destined for a career as a hairdresser.

Ronnie and I tack up Bessie, Penny, Everest and Soames.

"Who's going to do Snowstorm?" I ask, knowing we will both want to do it.

"You put the saddle on and I'll get the bridle," suggests Ronnie. She is quite clever at avoiding an argument.

Helen, the head girl, shows us where the brand new tack is and we admire it before approaching Snowstorm. She watches us curiously, her ears twitching back and forth, still getting accustomed to her new surroundings.

"Easy, girl," I whisper, patting her neck before sliding the saddle into position. She stands quietly while I tighten the girth.

"She seems very gentle," comments Ronnie, slipping the shiny new bit into the mare's mouth and doing up the noseband and throatlatch.

"She's wonderful," I sigh.

"Snowstorm's rider should be here by now. Maybe they won't turn up," says Ronnie hopefully.

We watch as the cavalcade of motley ponies and riders sets off for the field, with Helen leading.

"Well, whoever it is obviously isn't coming, so I'll ride Snowstorm down to the field in their place."

"Matty! You wouldn't dare!" Ronnie is horrified. "Miss Pugh will be furious!"

"You're probably right," I agree and for a moment

15

my nerve wavers. Then Snowstorm nickers gently and I gaze again into her huge, liquid brown eyes, and melt. I have to ride her, and this is such a perfect opportunity. I tell myself it's meant to be.

"You're crazy, Matty," Ronnie declares as I push my helmet on and grab the reins. Snowstorm stands perfectly still while I place my foot in the stirrup and land lightly in the saddle. I take one last look around to make sure that the absent student is nowhere to be seen. Then I squeeze Snowstorm's sides, much too hard (I'm used to well-worn riding school ponies) and she leaps forward, throwing me off balance for a moment. But I recover, realize she responds to light aids, and react accordingly.

"See you," I shout as Snowstorm sets off at a working trot.

"In the hospital, probably," yells Ronnie, and I just hear Gina, who's been watching from Elliot's stable, add, "Matty is going to be in BIG trouble."

My feelings are ping-ponging between fear of what Miss Pugh will do to me if she finds out, and the sheer pleasure of riding Snowstorm. She steps out enthusiastically, her head held high, her tail streaming. Her mouth is as soft as ice-cream, and I hardly have to touch the reins to check her. It's almost as if she reads my thoughts, and knows when I want her to slow down and speed up.

Now we've come to the end of the main road and are approaching the first of two busy streets that have to be crossed to get to the field. I feel confident that Snowstorm will be traffic-proof. Even so, when a noisy motorbike speeds towards the junction I begin to worry. Snowstorm lays back her ears and dances a little on the spot while we wait for a clear road before we can cross. I worry a bit more and this transmits down the reins and Snowstorm continues to fidget. Gina's words dominate my thoughts.

MATTY IS GOING TO BE IN BIG TROUBLE.

What if something awful happens and I get into an accident and poor Snowstorm is hurt? I would hate myself. I would never be forgiven, no one would ever want to be friends with me, and I wouldn't blame them. It would be my own fault. Why am I so impulsive? Ronnie has told me before that I should look before I leap, that I don't think enough.

I'm in danger of getting into a panic when suddenly the traffic clears and Snowstorm trots calmly across and down the street and over the next junction, and then we've reached the field. She stands quietly while I open the gate, and we see the class at the far end, all walking around in a circle. All my fears have vanished. I'm feeling pleased and excited, so much so, in fact, that I now do another very foolish thing. Instead of walking quietly over to join the class, counting myself lucky that I haven't been caught, I simply cannot resist the expanse of springy grass that stretches before me. So I ask Snowstorm for canter and she obliges instantly, her light, rhythmic stride covering the ground with ease. I'm in heaven.

We have done two perfect circles before I notice that an unfamiliar man in a gray suit wearing steel-rimmed glasses and a stony face is watching us. Next to him stands a boy who looks about fifteen, with black curly hair and immaculate riding clothes. He is glaring furiously. Instinct tells me to pull up, and they both run over to me, shouting.

"What the heck do you think you're doing?" growls the boy, grabbing Snowstorm's reins and practically pulling me out of the saddle.

"How dare you ride my pony without permission?"

Chapter 2

Snowstorm is blowing a little, and my face is so red it could be mistaken for a very large tomato. I can't think quickly enough to make up any valid excuse.

"I'm sorry," I burble. "I didn't realize. I thought she belonged to Miss Pugh."

"Well, you thought wrong, didn't you?" says the man in the suit, looking critically at Snowstorm, checking that I haven't done any damage. "I'll make sure Miss Pugh knows about his."

I am mortified. I didn't expect such an onslaught and have visions of being banned from the stables forever. My lip starts to tremble. The boy must have noticed and taken pity on me because although he still looks angry he says, "All right, Dad, I think she got the message. No harm done"

"No harm done! By sheer chance, I'd say. The mare could have been ruined by some silly kid…" And he continues for a good five minutes while the boy feels Snowstorm's legs and grunts that the stirrups are twisted and the throat lash is too loose.

"I'm sorry," I repeat, wishing the ground would open up and swallow me. The man seems to have tired of his tirade and says dismissively, "Oh, for goodness sake, go. But don't ever let me catch you near this pony again, understand?"

I skulk away, feeling two inches tall, even less. I hear him say, "Super little pony, worth every penny, Mark. She'll do us proud," and the boy replies obediently, "Yes, Dad."

I walk away without looking back, eventually passing the class, who are riding large circles at walk and trot. Thankfully, they are too far away to have heard or seen what has happened. I hope.

When I get back to the stables, Gina and Ronnie rush over to meet me.

"What happened? Did you get caught?" demands Gina.

"Just after you left, a car pulled up and this boy and his Dad came looking for Snowstorm," says Ronnie.

"You could have warned me," I say indignantly.

"We couldn't. There wasn't time," insists Gina.

"Well, you could have lied about where Snowstorm was," I add, feeling wretched. I am not prepared to admit that it's my own fault for taking Snowstorm without permission. I want some sympathy and Gina obliges.

"Poor Matty. Did they give you a hard time?"

"You could say that," I grunt.

To my surprise, Miss Pugh doesn't tear me to shreds for riding Snowstorm, so I assume that Mark and his father didn't complain about me after all. Even so, I make myself scarce in the feed room until I'm sure they're gone.

When I emerge, the others have congregated in the yard. I glare before anyone can make a silly remark. Even so, Gina says, "That Mark kid sure is good looking."

"Can't say I noticed," I mutter. "I was more interested in Snowstorm. I wish my parents had the money to buy her for me."

"Dream on," laughs Ronnie.

"My Mom and Dad could afford it, I think, but they encourage me to earn the things I want and not give me everything on a plate," says Spike. "I suppose they're right in the long run, but sometimes I just wish …"

There is a gloomy silence, which Gina suddenly fills with, "We're all doomed to be forever in a pony-less state. It's fate."

"No way," retorts Spike. "There's no such thing as fate."

"Maybe we should call ourselves The Pony-less Club. Or The No Pony Club."

"Defeatist," mutters Spike.

An argument is about to erupt, but I'm thinking about what Spike has said about earning the things you want.

"Be quiet, you two," I interrupt. "Spike has a point, you know."

"About what?" asks Ronnie.

"Individually, it doesn't look as if we could each have our own pony. Not at the moment," I venture.

"We know that," grunts Ronnie.

"But if we work together, pool our savings, and think of ways to earn money, there's no reason why we can't buy a pony together. It might take a little while, but –"

"A pony to share." Ronnie is smiling.

"It sounds like the title of a horsey book – *A Pony to Share*," repeats Gina, savoring the sound of the words.

"We could do it, I'm sure," I continue, "What do you think, Spike?"

She nods enthusiastically. "You're on. We just need to draw up our plan of action."

It sounds simple, doesn't it? If only acquiring a pony were really that easy, wouldn't we have one by now? Why haven't we thought of it before? Or perhaps it isn't going to be so easy after all.

We are now sitting in the stable yard, at the far corner by the fence where there's shade from the glare of the afternoon sun. Ronnie, efficient as always, is wielding a pencil and large sheet of paper, which she stole from the clipboard hanging in the office.

"Timetable," she announces briskly. "We need a timetable with a target deadline for P Day."

"What's P Day?" asks Gina.

"Pony Day. When we go out and buy our pony."

"Oh. Shouldn't we decide how much money we need to save first?"

"Gina has a point," agrees Spike. "How much?"

"It depends on what sort of pony we intend to get," I suggest.

"Well, obviously it isn't going to be an expensive pedigree thoroughbred," observes Gina, pushing a strand of blonde hair out of her eyes. She has delicate features and pale blue eyes and looks so fragile that sometimes I think a gust of wind would knock her over.

"Why not? We could get a retired racehorse," says Spike, and I see that she's imagining herself galloping across the moors, the wind in her ears.

"I don't want an old horse," moans Ronnie.

"Ageist," teases Spike.

"We could buy a colt and break it in," says Gina. "A beautiful chestnut with four white socks and a white star. We could call him Coppergold."

"I want a nice Welsh cob, sensible but with plenty of zip. Preferably dun. Dun is my favorite color," muses Ronnie.

"Or an Appaloosa. I'd love an Appaloosa. They look so striking and they have great temperaments, according to what I've read," continues Spike.

"I'd like a gray mare, like Snowstorm," I add wistfully.

"You just want Snowstorm. You have to forget it, Matty. She's a really expensive pony and Mark would NEVER sell her to you, particularly not after what happened today." Ronnie's voice is sympathetic but firm, and I'm reminded of my mother for a moment.

"We can't always have what we want, Matty," Mom tells me frequently. I always reply, "Why not?"

"Don't you think we're getting a bit carried away?" asks Gina. "The time to argue about what sort of pony to get will be when we have the money."

"I think we're going around in circles," laughs Ronnie, pretending to pull her hair out. "Look, we all know roughly what kind of amount is needed to buy a decent sort of pony, say fourteen hands or so, about seven years old, safe, well-schooled."

I nod. "Yes, we've all looked through the For Sale ads in the pony mags plenty of times, imagining which ponies we would like to buy."

"Right. So let's agree on an approximate figure to aim for. Then we need to work out how much capital we can put in and how much more we'll need to earn to make up the total."

"Capital?" jokes Spike, mimicking Ronnie's voice. "You sound like a high powered businesswoman, Ronnie. Can't you speak the same language as the rest of us?" (She often makes fun of Ronnie's present career aim, which is to open a chain of successful vegetarian fast food restaurants, sell them, and retire at twenty-one on the profits. We're all convinced that this is a non-starter, but there's no telling Ronnie sometimes.)

"All right, you uneducated bunch. Savings. How much have we got?"

The next five minutes reveal that between us we can barely raise a quarter of what we need; considerably less, in fact.

"So what about the rest? How are we going to earn it? Suggestions, anyone?" Ronnie is still using her authoritarian voice and Spike is getting a bit irritated. We are all aware of how very hot it has become, and I wonder how productive this meeting will be if we sit in the sun for much longer.

Suddenly, Gina interjects with, "Where will we keep our pony? Surely not here, at Miss Pugh's stables?"

"Where else would you suggest?" says Spike impatiently.

"Let's stick to the point, shall we?" glares Ronnie. "We're supposed to be sorting out how to earn the money we need."

So we draw up a list of things we can do for ready cash. It is a laborious process, but we think of the following:

Babysitting (not popular with anyone)

Delivering newspapers (although we're not sure if we're old enough to do this yet – Spike is going to check)

Gardening

Cleaning Cars

Dog walking (would anyone pay us for this?)

Car wash (but we would have to enlist the help of an adult for this)

"It's not a very inspiring list," remarks Gina gloomily.

"My parents will pay me for doing household chores, like the ironing and vacuuming," says Spike, determined to be positive. "Plus other things they hate doing, like cleaning the bath or the toilet."

"I don't think my parents would pay me for cleaning the toilet," observes Ronnie.

27

"Or mine," I add, and we start to giggle.

"We have to keep thinking of other things we can do. It's an ongoing process," says Ronnie. "Would it be realistic to aim to have enough money by Christmas?"

"What, in the Year 2020?" jokes Spike.

"No," replies Ronnie curtly.

"We could aim for this Christmas," I suggest. "We can extend our deadline if things go badly. But it's important to have a date to aim for."

"I agree," nods Gina.

"Good," says Spike. "Now, I vote that we all head for the town swimming pool before we melt!"

I must say it feels wonderful to dive into cool water at long last, even though we have to fight through hordes of children to find a space. That's the trouble with the public pool in summer – it's full of noisy kids! (As you'll gather, I don't include myself in this category.) When I'm rich I'm going to have a private pool in the back yard, so I can swim whenever I like and invite all my friends over to share the fun.

When we board the local bus to take us home several hours later, we're all very refreshed and in better moods, if somewhat hungry (except for Ronnie, who has consumed three ice-creams and now feels sick. We aren't sympathetic, as she eats and eats and never seems to put on any weight).

We chatter on as we usually do for the entire trip back, but in the occasional pauses, I'm sure we're all imagining what it will be like to have our own pony. We each have our ideal fantasy pony, and I must admit that I'm somewhat fixated on Snowstorm. Riding her today really triggered something inside me. I have fallen completely in love.

There's a new movie playing at the town center theater the next day, and we decide to go to the evening showing. It stars our favorite heartthrob actor and has had great reviews. It's also set on an island full of wild horses, which is an added bonus.

"You smell like chlorine," remarks Mom as I walk into the kitchen.

"Hmm," I respond vaguely. "What's for dinner?"

"Salad and pizza," she replies. "You'd better give me that wet towel to put in the laundry. I rummage in my bag and produce said item.

"You'll never guess what," I begin, taking lettuce and tomatoes out of the fridge.

"What?" asks Mom dutifully. "Miss Pugh finally sold her land to the developers?"

"No, there's a gorgeous new pony at the stables, a renter. The boy who owns her is a real jerk, and his Dad is even worse." My tone is bitter and whiny. "It's so unfair. He doesn't deserve a pony. He can't ride properly." (Okay, I haven't seen him ride but I just have this instinct.)

"Well, there's no point worrying about it, hon." She gestures to me to sit down and Dad joins us. "Now, eat your pizza before it gets cold."

For some reason, I find it difficult to sleep. Maybe it's the heat, or maybe I ate too much pizza. Anyway, my head is filled with images of Snowstorm. And, to my annoyance, Mark.

At 11:30 I hear Mom and Dad come upstairs to bed. I throw open the bedroom window and stare blankly at our little back yard, with its neat flower borders and shrubs, lovingly tended by Dad, the rock garden that he built with Mom, and the newly mown lawn. I can't help wishing that it's a nice big paddock with white post and rail fencing and a running stream; or perhaps a lush orchard with apple trees and green grass. Either way, in my fantasy there's a gray pony grazing contentedly at one end, and when I look out she peers up at me and greets me with a friendly whinny.

With this pleasant thought in mind, I get back into bed (or rather onto the bed – it's too hot to lie under the covers) and drift into a deep sleep. I dream that I'm reliving my ride on Snowstorm, only this time we're galloping, and I'm riding bareback, and all I can hear is the sound of her hooves drumming. It's a thrilling experience and I know that I will never ride a pony as good as this one. Then suddenly I hear a familiar voice yelling at me, and my stomach lurches. I look over my shoulder and see Mark's Dad running after me, shouting that he'll kill me when he catches me. I urge Snowstorm on faster, and when I next look over my shoulder I am being pursued by a car, and Mark is driving it with his face set and his eyes blazing and wild, like someone possessed. Now the car is level with Snowstorm's shoulder and I'm breathing hard, my mouth dry, and Snowstorm is racing faster than I would have thought possible. Then the car window opens and Mark throws something at me and the next thing I know, I am falling, falling, hitting the ground, and it hurts all over. But even so, I get back up and, when I look around, Snowstorm is being led into a truck and she is rearing and panicking.

"Stop!" I scream and throw myself at Mark, but he pushes me over and laughs in my face. Then the truck speeds away and I'm watching, helpless, as it disappears, and all I can hear is the haunting, high-pitched whinny coming from inside as Snowstorm is taken from me.

Chapter 3

"Do you think this new dress looks good on me? I mean, really. Be honest." Gina's eyes search my face for the answer she wants to hear.

"It looks great, Gina. Really," I reply.

"You don't think it's too garish? I mean, red can be a really dominant color."

"It's great, Gina."

"And you don't look at all like a big chili pepper," adds Spike.

Gina thumps her and they giggle. I join in, but truthfully my mind is miles away and I'm not that interested in Gina's new dress.

We're sitting on a bus on the way in to town to see the movie I mentioned before. It's a lovely night, warm and clear, I'm in good company with my favorite people, and tomorrow is the start of summer vacation. There are lots of reasons to be cheerful. So why do I feel so moody?

I suppose the day didn't exactly get off to a good start. When I awoke from my awful dream about Snowstorm, I fell back into a heavy sleep, which meant I overslept, since I had forgotten to set my alarm clock and neither Mom nor Dad bothered to wake me up. When I went downstairs, frustrated and irritable, they were sitting in the back yard, sunning themselves in deck chairs and smiling benignly.

When I arrived at the stables it was deserted. Everyone – and I mean everyone – had gone out for a ride. Yes, a family of four had cancelled at the last minute, having come down with a stomach bug, so four ponies were free and Miss Pugh, in a rare fit of generosity, had decreed that her little helpers could ride in their place. (I learned all this later, when Gina, Spike and Ronnie returned, looking rather smug, I thought.) So, I had missed out on a free ride because I was so late arriving.

Anyway, finding the place empty I found Gina's radio in the tack room, put on a dance music station and sat and sulked. I soon got bored with this, though, and decided to see if I could find a pony to talk to. Elliott, the skewbald with the brillo-pad mane, was dozing in his stall, still tacked up (I later learned that I could have ridden him on the trail ride). So I loosened his girth and patted him for a bit, until I heard a whinny coming from Snowstorm's stall. She was so friendly, nuzzling my hair and licking my hands, that my heart did a little leap.

Here we were, alone together. It would have been so easy to take her out for a ride. And I would have loved to, but I didn't dare. So, instead, I contented myself with chatting to her about my morning, and asking her if she knew what my dream meant. Of course, she just listened patiently, nodding politely from time to time. I had just started to tell her about the movie we were going to see that night when I heard someone coughing behind me and I realized we were being watched. I turned sharply. You guessed it; my friend Mark.

"Please, go on," he said, clearly amused, although not to the point of managing a smile. I blushed furiously, wondering how long he had been standing there. He must have thought I was crazy. Then I remembered his father's warning about never going near Snowstorm and here I was, standing in the stable with her. Mark must have read my thoughts because he said, "Don't worry, Dad's not with me today. Just as well, really."

I assumed that he meant just as well for me. There was an awkward silence, filled only by the inane jabbering of the deejay on the radio station. Then Mark said, "Would you mind showing me where her tack is?"

Now it was my turn to make fun of him. I pretended to concentrate hard before saying, "Well, I might be making a stab in the dark, but I think it's just possible that it might be in the tack room."

Mark's face took on the stony stare of the previous day and for a brief second, I regretted my sarcasm.

"Over there," I said rudely, pointing in the direction of the tack room. I had no intention of showing him. "Yours will be the new stuff."

I sat on an upturned bucket, watching him tack up, determined not to help, not that he needed it, of course. He took Snowstorm into the ring and practiced transitions, followed by a very impressive serpentine. Then he dismounted and spent ages putting up a small course of jumps from the assorted poles, oil drums and tires. He was getting very sweaty, and glared at me once or twice but I just glared back. Maybe he thought I should have helped.

Anyway, Snowstorm was a great little jumper, really game and careful, and they jumped several fluent rounds, from different directions. Mark rode well, I had to admit, but there was something sort of mechanical about the way he rode. He wasn't mean or anything, but it was almost like watching a machine. After about an hour he walked Snowstorm to cool her down and then untacked and groomed her. By then, I could hear the riders coming back, so I got up to open the gates.

"Hey, Matty. Where did you go? We had a great ride," announced Spike, who was at the front of the cavalcade.

"Yes, we even had a gallop," added Ronnie. "You should have seen Soames go."

"You missed out this time, Matty," said Gina, and I thought, all right, do you have to rub salt in the wound? "Miss Pugh was in such a good mood today. She went out to lunch. She's probably still there now. So, where were you?"

Then she saw Mark leaving Snowstorm's stall. "Oh, I see," she said in a knowing voice. "Matty, you didn't –"

"Didn't what!" I exclaimed indignantly.

"Ride Snowstorm again, of course, what did you think she meant?" retorted Spike. "My, you are defensive today."

Mark swept past us as if we didn't exist and disappeared into the yard. I think he turned to look back at one point, but I might have imagined it.

"Penny for them?" asks Ronnie, and I snap out of my daydream.

"Sorry?"

"Penny for your thoughts," she repeats.

I think that is such an irritating expression.

"Nothing to tell," I reply.

"Do you think Gina likes Mark?" she says suddenly, and before I can think of a reply, the bus pulls up outside our grungy old movie theater, which has yet to be converted into a multiplex.

We all enjoy the movie, and the lead actor is gorgeous, but, for me, the best thing about it is the horses; lots of them. The main one, the stallion, is magnificent, and when he jumps over the cliff at the end to swim back to his island I'm almost in tears. (But I won't say any more to spoil the ending in case you go to see it.)

As usual, there is a big line for the ladies room afterwards (why do the men's toilets never have lines?) and we are the last ones in. Gina insists on spending forever touching up her makeup and trying to get a stain out of her new red dress where Spike dropped chocolate ice cream on it, so we all wait with her until Ronnie says, impatiently, "Oh, hurry up Gina. I want pizza before we go home, and we don't have much time left before the last bus."

Gina finishes dabbing at her dress with a paper towel while we drag her off to the takeout across the road. Of course, as we are last out of the movies we now have to join the line at the takeout. Spike keeps looking anxiously at her watch. "If we don't get a move on, we'll miss that bus."

"Well, I want that pizza," insists Ronnie, an edge to her voice. "And we've got a whole five minutes."

At that very moment we glance through the window to see the bus pulling away from the stop.

"Oh, that's great," Spike mutters angrily. "That was the last bus."

"It can't be," says Ronnie.

"Well, it was. Are you satisfied now?" Spike sounds irritated. "You wouldn't listen."

By now, Ronnie has her pizza, and while she munches we crowd around the timetable at the bus stop.

"We forgot about the summer schedule, didn't we?" realizes Gina. "They changed the bus times yesterday. *Now* what do we do?"

"We could get a taxi, I suppose," suggests Ronnie.

"Or walk home," says Spike. "It's not that far."

"Do you think we ought to call our parents, and tell them what happened?" I wonder.

"No credit left on my cell phone," says Ronnie, "So I left it at home."

"Same here," says Gina.

Mine is tucked safely in my pocket, still switched off from when we were in the theater. I curl my hand around it.

Spike glares. "Surely we're old enough to take care of ourselves? Anyway, my parents will probably be in bed by now. It's nearly eleven thirty."

"But is it safe?" says Gina nervously.

"It isn't a long walk," insists Ronnie, downing the last piece of pizza with great relish. "We'll only be an hour late."

"If we take a shortcut, we'll hardly be late at all," grins Spike.

"What shortcut?" I ask anxiously, and the others start to giggle.

We're halfway across the graveyard when I start to have my doubts.

"I don't think much of this shortcut, Spike," I begin.

We're weaving a path through crumbling tombstones and overgrown graves. Every horror film I've ever seen starts to flash into my mind and I feel a shiver down my spine as I imagine skeletal fingers pushing through the earth to exert an icy grip on my ankle or, worse, flesh-eating zombies emerging suddenly from their resting places. "We shouldn't be here," I say.

"You don't believe in ghosts, surely?" mocks Spike.

"Of course not," I respond, keeping my voice as casual as possible. "But it's so dark and I keep hearing weird hooting sounds –"

"Owls," says Ronnie.

"Whatever. Anyway, I hope you know your way, because Gina is really worried."

I glance at Gina, and in fact she seems to have bucked up quite a bit and doesn't look scared at all.

"What's that noise?" I hiss suddenly.

"Owls, I told you," repeats Ronnie.

"No. This was different. Footsteps. Coming from over there."

"For goodness sake, Matty, get a grip –" begins Spike as the church bells strike midnight.

And then we see it, standing right in front of us – this large dark shape blocking our path.

"Is that what I think it is?" mutters Ronnie in disbelief.

We all nod in agreement.

"Definitely," I say. "It's definitely a horse."

Chapter 4

The horse comes toward us until I can feel his breath on my face, warm and welcoming. He regards us curiously, his eyes wide, and I notice a little cut above his right eyebrow, where the blood has dried.

"Easy there," I whisper, anxious not to scare him. "Gina, give me your scarf."

"What?" Gina clutches her long floral silk scarf protectively.

"We need something to hold him with. It's for a good cause."

Reluctantly, Gina hands it over and I slip it over the horse's head. He seems quite happy to be caught, even relieved.

Ronnie and Spike stroke his neck and he gives a friendly nicker.

"He's gorgeous," sighs Gina.

"So, what do we do with him?" wonders Spike.

"Take him home, I suppose," I suggest, and we all agree.

The horse walks beside us quietly, his ears flicking back and forth at our chatter as we speculate on where he came from. It feels unreal, walking down our terraced street with a horse in the pale moonlight.

I study the horse's graceful neck and long, sloping shoulders and admire his aristocratic head. I consider his deep girth, strong back and powerful quarters, his long legs and neat feet. He's a very dark bay, with a distinctive white marking on his face shaped like a crescent moon.

The question is, what was he doing in the grave-yard at midnight?

"Matty, where on earth have you been? We were getting worried; Ronnie's parents have been around here already to see if you'd gotten back, and Gina's mother has been on the phone three times. We told them to wait a while longer before calling the police."

My parents are sitting in the kitchen, looking anxious, and I feel guilty for not calling them.

"Mind you, we're used to you getting into situations," says my father. "So what happened this time?"

"We missed the last bus so we walked home. I'm sorry if you were worried. I should have phoned," And I glare pointedly at Spike. "Then we found a horse in the graveyard," thinking how unlikely this last bit sounded. "We brought him back with us. He's in the back yard."

"Oh." My father considers this for a minute, peers outside, and then says, "You girls keep an eye on him, while I fetch some rope out of the garage."

. He reappears with a coil of soft white rope, which we soon turn into a makeshift halter. Gina is pleased to get her scarf back.

Then my mother produces a tasty-looking apple for the horse. "Good thinking," I nod approvingly, wondering if my parents do indeed possess some kind of horsy potential after all. I hold out the apple and the horse expresses an interest almost immediately. He pokes his nose forward and very gently grazes his velvety lips on my hand to take the tasty morsel, which he munches noisily.

"I'd love to stay here with the horse, but I think I'd better get back home," says Ronnie.

"Yes, I think so," agrees my mother.

"Same here," says Spike and despite her protestations that she is perfectly capable of walking home, Dad insists on driving her back.

"What about you, Gina?" My Mom has noticed that Gina is looking very worried. She knows what Gina's mother can be like.

"What am I going to tell her?" says Gina anxiously.

"The truth, of course," I reply. "That the last bus left early, so we missed it and had to walk home."

Gina frowns and Mom says, "Tell you what, why don't you stay here for the night, Gina? You look tired. You can go back home tomorrow. I can call your mother and explain things."

"Oh, would you?" Gina responds gratefully. "She's so difficult to talk to when she gets all worked up."

So Mom does her bit and manages to calm down Gina's mother while we drink soda and discuss what to do with the horse.

"It's far too late to call the police," I insist. Thankfully, Dad says, "You're probably right. We'll think about it in the morning."

"It *is* the morning," I point out.

"True." Dad yawns. "We'd better get to bed."

Gina and I check first that the horse is all right. He's tethered to the fence and has a bucket of fresh water to drink. I've bathed the cut above his eye with water and antiseptic and he looks reasonably contented.

It's hard to sleep when you have a strange horse outside in the back yard and Gina snoring away in a sleeping bag on the floor but, eventually, I drift off and am awakened at 7:30 by the sound of someone's car alarm going off. (This is a frequent occurrence.) I turn on the radio and get ready to shower. Then I remember, and rush to the window. Yes, the horse is still there, resting a hind leg and looking bored.

Mom and Dad are sitting at the kitchen table, and it's obvious they've been discussing what to do about our nocturnal visitor. I pour myself a glass of milk and explain that Gina, amazingly, is still asleep.

"Your mother has already phoned the police and reported that the horse is here," my father says. I feel a wave of panic. Mom notices my reaction and, realizing I'm disappointed that we might lose the horse so soon, adds hastily, "But no one around here has reported him missing yet. So it seems that for now

47

it's up to us to decide what to do with him. I think the police hope that we'll sort something out."

Dad smiles wryly. "They have enough to do without trying to deal with stray horses. Anyway, we've done the right thing by reporting it."

"That means we can keep him, until someone claims him," I say, excitement rising.

"It isn't that simple," Mom replies. "I mean, we can't keep a horse in the back yard. And who's going to pay for his food and vet bills?"

"We will," I say undeterred. I have a horse. At last, I have a horse!

"We?" Dad's eyebrows go up and there's a hint of a frown.

"I mean Ronnie and Spike and Gina and I. We have pocket money and savings."

"I'm not sure I'm very happy about that," says Mom. "And you still haven't addressed the issue of where to keep him."

"At Miss Pugh's stables, of course," I reply, full of enthusiasm.

"You haven't asked her. What if there isn't space?"

"There will be," I insist, refusing to be thwarted. Nothing is going to stop me now that I'm the proud owner of a beautiful horse. (Okay. So perhaps I'm getting a bit carried away.)

The horse gives a little whinny and Ronnie's grinning face appears at the open doorway.

"Great morning," she declares.

She accepts Mom's offer of a glass of juice. Since Gina still hasn't made an appearance by the time we finish our second glass, I decide to go and wake her.

"I'll go," offers Ronnie. "I've always wanted to see Gina without her makeup!"

Before Mom and Dad leave for work, Mom insists that we go straight to Miss Pugh's to ask if we can keep the horse at her stables for the time being, and we promise to do this once we get Gina out of bed.

We complete the ten minute walk there in less than five minutes and arrive hot, sweaty and out of breath. Needless to say, Miss Pugh is nowhere to be seen. One of the junior helpers (the youngest is seven) says, helpfully, "She might be in the top field checking a fence. Elliott got out again last night and was found wandering in the housing development this morning. The lady who runs the residents association turned up with him an hour ago, really angry. Says Miss Pugh should take better care of her ponies."

"Too right," agrees Ronnie.

"Is Elliot okay?" I ask.

She nods. "Oh, he's fine, but Miss Pugh is in a foul mood. I wouldn't bother her right now if I were you."

We thank her for the warning, but agree that we have to tackle Miss Pugh about our horse as soon as possible.

We track her down in the top field as expected. She's trying to repair the broken fence with a bale of string. It doesn't look very effective.

"Would you like some help?" I offer cheerfully, in an attempt to get on her good side.

She scowls. "This is beyond help. I'll have to pay to have it repaired properly, I suppose, if I want to keep that old bat from the housing development off my back."

Ronnie looks at me as if to say, "Let's come back later," but I go ahead regardless and tell her about our mystery horse.

When I've finished she says, "And I suppose you want to keep him here until his owner turns up?"

I nod.

To my surprise she says, "No. Definitely not."

"But why? We'll pay for his keep and look after him. You take boarders. I don't understand."

"Because he might be stolen. I can't harbor a stolen horse."

"But he isn't stolen. He's with us." I protest.

"How do you know he isn't stolen? You don't. It's bound to spell trouble, and I have enough problems on my hands without you adding to them. Besides, I don't have any room."

"But –" Ronnie begins and then stops, seeing that it's useless to argue. We walk away and I say, "Maybe she'll be in a better mood later on."

Ronnie is not convinced.

"What do we do now?" I wonder. "There are no other riding stables for miles. And no local boarding stables."

"We're stuck."

"No, we're not," I argue. "We just can't think of anywhere yet. That doesn't mean there isn't somewhere else to try."

"Spike might have a few ideas," suggests Gina, trying to sound positive.

As we leave, I notice Mark schooling Snowstorm in

the corner of the small field. I turn away, but Gina can't help watching him.

I remember my dream ride on Snowstorm and wonder what it will feel like to ride the dark bay. At this moment, I am absolutely determined that somewhere, somehow, we'll find a way to keep him.

We haven't been given this gift horse only to lose him again. He's meant to be ours. It's fate.

Chapter 5

By now, Spike has joined us and we're walking along the road in stony silence. I feel strange inside. Normally today would be spent at the stables, working hard as usual and having a laugh with friends, maybe even getting a ride if we're lucky. And here we are, with a horse of our own (temporarily, I know) feeling miserable when we should be ecstatic.

"If we can't keep him at Miss Pugh's, where can we keep him?" wonders Ronnie. "There really isn't anywhere else for miles. This area is so built up with houses and industrial parks."

"No farms, no other stables, no fields. It's no wonder there are so few horse owners." I feel more downcast than ever.

"But there *has* to be somewhere. We can't give up."

Ronnie is adamant. "In the meantime, let's all go back to Matty's house. The horse might give us inspiration."

"As soon as Mom hears that Miss Pugh won't take him, we might as well kiss him goodbye," I moan. "We can't keep him in our yard, so the police will have to take him away and find someone else to look after him, maybe a horse rescue place or animal sanctuary."

"What if no one claims him? Will he have to be destroyed?" wonders Gina, adding to our gloom.

"Of course not," says Spike uncertainly. "It isn't like finding a lost dog, you know."

"So what does happen?" Gina persists and Spike says impatiently. "Oh, honestly, Gina," and we all decide not to pursue it.

Before we push open my garden gate Spike suddenly whispers, "Don't say anything yet about not finding somewhere to keep this horse. We need more time."

"It's all right; Mom and Dad will still be at work." Dad works in the city, and Mom does a job share at the local town hall with someone named Angie, working two full days and three half days. Today is a full day. However, when we go into the kitchen there she is, loading up the washing machine.

"Mom, you're home already," I say, trying not to sound too disappointed.

"Yes, dear. Angie wants tomorrow afternoon off so I agreed to change shifts with her." Of course, the next thing she says is, "Did you sort things out with Miss Pugh? Has she got space for another horse?"

All eyes are focused on me. My mind races. Then I reply, "She wasn't there. She had to go out. We're going back later to ask her."

We all give a mental sigh of relief and I get cans of soda out of the fridge and take them outside, where Gina is now swooning over the horse.

"He's gorgeous." The horse eyes her curiously but seems unperturbed by so much attention.

"He's kind of old, I'd say," remarks Spike, studying him. "But he's very handsome."

"I think we should call him Phantom," sighs Gina.

"How unoriginal," says Spike. "Just because we found him in a graveyard."

"Anyway, it's a bit premature to give him a name, isn't it?" adds Ronnie cautiously, and I wish she wasn't such a killjoy sometimes.

"How could anyone not realize that they lost a horse like this?" wonders Gina.

"Well, it can't be anyone around here, since this is such an un-horsy area," adds Spike.

"Maybe he traveled a long way."

"He doesn't look like a horse that's been on the road for a long time, Gina," Spike replies.

"He could have been stolen," suggests Ronnie.

At this point I've had enough of speculation. "Look, we've got to sort out this accommodation problem," I say in a low voice. "And fast. Any ideas?"

Needless to say, a fruitless half hour follows, by which time we're getting on each other's nerves. I'm actually relieved when Spike says, "I really have to get back to the stables. I promised to take a group out after lunch, and I want to eat my sandwich first and get ready. Sorry to desert you all."

"Okay. We'll see you later then, back here?" I reply and she nods.

My Mom peers out of the kitchen and says, "Do you girls want to stay for lunch? It's only salad and quiche, but there's plenty of it."

"Yes, thank you, Mrs. Mathews," says Gina, who likes both my parents and says they are far more laid-back than her mother. (Mind you, I imagine most people are.)

A look of horror crosses Ronnie's face. "What time is it?"

"Nearly one o'clock," I reply.

"Oh, no! I promised Mom I'd baby-sit the twins today so she could meet Dad for a special lunch. It's their wedding anniversary."

"You'd better get going, then," we reply sympathetically, and Ronnie makes a hasty getaway.

Gina seems to enjoy having lunch with Mom and me, having cleared it with her own mother first, but I'm still preoccupied about where to keep the bay horse. I suppose it had never occurred to me that Miss Pugh would say no. Maybe Ronnie's right; maybe I should go back and try her again later. She might change her mind.

After lunch, Gina and I decide to take the horse out for a stroll. The rope halter seems secure and we stand at either side of his head, in case of problems. He moves nicely, though Gina notices that he's a little stiff on the nearside when he trots. But he holds his head so proudly and watches everything that's going on, his ears twitching, nostrils sniffing the air, and I feel a wave of pride. This is what it feels like to have our own horse, I tell myself. It's a great feeling and I don't want to have it taken away. I look across at Gina and we smile, sharing the moment.

I look thoughtfully at the row of garages for rent on the edge of the housing estate and wonder if they could be adapted to make a stable.

"I wish there was another riding school around here," says Gina. "Miss Pugh has a captive market, so she has no incentive to improve things."

"You sound like Ronnie," I smile, reminded of Ronnie's penchant for business language. "But you're right. And if there was another stable, we could keep our horses there and have proper lessons."

It's later than I realize when we get back.

"I'd better get home soon," says Gina nervously. "Or Mom will think I don't want to go home at all."

Mom is weeding the rock garden when we return. "Nice time, dear?" she asks.

I nod and anticipate the next question.

"Sort things out with Miss Pugh, did you?"

"She's still out," I lie, stalling for time. I wonder what the point is – sooner or later Mom will know the real situation. We can't keep the horse in our yard for another night. Ronnie's yard is the same size as ours, and Gina's Mom would be horrified at the idea of a horse in *her* yard. And Spike's parents are both allergic to grass so their garden is Japanese style with soft white gravel in swirly patterns and a little pond with a bridge. I'm about to admit failure when Spike comes crashing through the gate, her face flushed, her voice full of excitement.

"It's all sorted out," she says confidently. "The horse has been booked in."

"So you got to see Miss Pugh after all? She was still out when these two called." My Mom sounds puzzled.

"Oh." Spike quickly assesses the situation. "Well, she just got back and it's all arranged."

"Thank goodness," sighs Gina, but I'm very sur- prised. I need to question Spike further so I suggest that the three of us go up to my room. As soon as the door closes Gina says, "How did you get Miss Pugh to change her mind?"

Spike grins. "I didn't."

"So what's going on, Spike?" I demand.

"The bay horse won't be staying with Miss Pugh," she admits.

I groan. "So we're back to square one. The perfect end to a perfect day."

"Don't be so defeatist," says Spike. "I said I've fixed it, and I have."

"So where will the horse be going?" I ask.

Spike smiles mysteriously. "Somewhere we never would have dreamed of."

Chapter 6

At least our horse seems reasonably happy with his new home, which is more than can be said for Gina and me. Still, Spike and Ronnie both think it's a great idea.

It's early evening, and we've just arrived at the old fort.

"I remembered seeing it in the distance when we were on that trail ride yesterday," Spike had explained to us on the way. "I'd never really noticed it before. No one ever comes here, so it'll be our secret. It used to be the quarters for the soldier's horses, so it has proper stables."

"Maybe, Spike, you would like to tell us why no one ever comes here," Gina inquires innocently.

Spike laughs. "Because some feeble-minded people seem to think it's haunted."

Only Ronnie giggles.

Now that we can see the fort in its full glory, I admit to being somewhat overawed by the spectacle. It's huge, constructed of graying brick that looks very solid in some places and crumbling in others. There's a proper stable yard framed by a semicircle of ten large archways, which each house three stalls. Assorted plants and weeds seem to spring from every crack in the brickwork, and the main archway is overgrown. It has a kind of sad splendor, and I imagine smartly-groomed military horses looking over their open half-doors. In its day it would have been magnificent.

Our horse suddenly lifts his head and whinnies, as if greeting the horses that once had been there. It feels a bit eerie.

"Let's get him bedded down," says Ronnie in a bossy voice.

Spike has "borrowed" a bag of shavings from Miss Pugh's stables, as well as large handfuls of pony treats. She chooses a suitable stable, which seems remarkably intact considering the place has been derelict for so long, and we all set about clearing and cleaning, and pulling out any plants we know to be poisonous.

It's a long job and it's starting to get dark by the time we're finished.

"What ghost is supposed to haunt this place?" asks Gina, trying to sound casual.

"A headless horseman," says Ronnie dismissively.

Gina goes pale.

"She's kidding," Spike reassures her. "It is a horse, though. Oddly enough, a dark bay, just like the one we found." Her voice has adopted a mysterious tone. "The horse we found in the graveyard. As the clock struck midnight."

Silence follows.

"Stop it, Spike," says Gina.

"It's true," insists Spike. "The horse belonged to Mad Major Wilkins. It would jump anything – walls topped with broken glass, rings of fire – even level crossing gates in the path of oncoming trains. I've been doing some research."

"So what happened?"

Spike lowers her voice mysteriously. "No one knows for sure. One dark night, the Major went out riding in a terrible storm. The wind was howling, the rain was beating down and there wasn't a shaft of moonlight to light the way as he left the safety of the

63

fort. Some said the Major was drunk, and he urged his horse to take one leap too many – over the edge of the quarry. Others say he was struck by lightning. One old soldier, who was on his way back from a bar, claimed he encountered the fearful pair on the road, and that the demonic horse threw his rider and trampled him to death, the bloodcurdling screams ringing in the night. Then, before his very eyes, a strange and ghostly mist descended, engulfing the Mad Major and his horse in its eerie glow. They were never seen again. Man and beast just disappeared."

Spike pauses for dramatic effect and I wish I didn't feel an icy chill on my spine.

Gina isn't sure whether or not to believe her, and I must admit I have my doubts. Still, it's an intriguing, if scary, tale.

"It's late," says Ronnie suddenly. "Let's get back."

I nod. My Mom and Ronnie's Mom have both gone to their Aerobics class, and Dad has gone out with a friend, so I've promised faithfully that I won't be too late getting back.

"OK," Spike agrees. "But before we go, we ought to name our horse, don't you think? And I have the perfect name for him."

"You're full of ideas today," Ronnie comments. "But go on. Tell us the name."

Spike smiles and says, "Moonlight. We found him in the moonlight, and he has a moon-shape on his forehead. It's perfect."

Ronnie and I agree that it is a good name.

As we walk away I look back over my shoulder at the fort in the gathering darkness, partially shrouded by shadows. It looks kinda creepy. Those people who believe in the supernatural, which, of course, I don't, claim that animals can sense evil, and since Moonlight seems perfectly at ease here, what is there to worry about?

"Let's talk about something nice," I suggest. "The County Show, for instance. Are any of us going to enter any classes?"

"I'd love to," Ronnie replies. "It depends on whether or not Miss Pugh will lend me Everest. I'd like to ride him in the showing class."

"I bet Mark will beat everyone in the jumping. Snowstorm is such a great pony," says Gina.

"I intend to enter the jumping class on Soames. He's the only decent jumper at the stables. What about you, Matty?" asks Spike.

I feel irritated at the thought of Mark riding Snowstorm, but I smile. "I don't need to borrow a horse, not when we've got our own."

"Oh, Matty, surely you can't be thinking what I think you're thinking? It's crazy to make plans about Moonlight. He doesn't belong to us."

I know she's right, but I can't help hoping.

The next few days are made in heaven. We all divide our time between Miss Pugh's stables and the old fort. No one has claimed Moonlight, and I decide to try to ride him.

"Be careful," warns Gina, as she helps me put the old bridle on Moonlight that Spike has borrowed from the stables. (Honestly, Spike is a devil when it comes to borrowing things.) We adjust the noseband and tighten the throatlatch and knot the broken reins. Ronnie leads Moonlight to the mounting block and holds him while I mount.

"I'm sure it'll be fine." I assure everyone. "He's very gentle and friendly. He must have been handled a great deal."

Then I'm sitting astride Moonlight, bareback, and not at all nervous. I have great confidence in him, and

66

it proves to be justified. He walks on when I nudge his sides, and when we've been around the yard at walk and trot twice, Ronnie lets go and leaves us to it. Seeing that we're not likely to encounter too many problems, Ronnie opens the gate to the field and Spike and Gina follow and watch as I try a short canter. Although I'm not overly crazy about riding bareback, I do prefer to ride without stirrups, finding it easier to feel the contact around the horse's sides. Moonlight has a nice springy canter, and a sweet temperament, and it's not long before my friends are shouting, "Me next, I want to have a turn!" like petulant children. After a while, I give in, and the others take turns to have a short ride each.

Finally, we agree that we've taxed Moonlight enough for one day, although he seems quite happy to go on.

We sit on the grass and let Moonlight graze while we eat a picnic lunch. Then Gina says that she has to go home, because her mother wants to take her shopping this afternoon, and Spike decides to go with her, as she has a dental appointment later on and doesn't want to be late. So Ronnie and I sunbathe for a while, listening to the radio, and I'm glad to be alive.

We must have dozed off for a while, because the next thing I know, Ronnie is shaking me furiously saying, "It's nearly seven thirty, and I'm supposed to be home babysitting the terrible twins so Mom and Dad can go out tonight."

I get to my feet and grab my backpack. Then I notice that Moonlight is nowhere to be seen.

"He can't be far," says Ronnie.

"No, he can't be far," I repeat, my heart sinking.

"The field is fenced in. He must be here somewhere."

We look and look, and whistle and call, but there's no sign of Moonlight.

"Oh, great, this is just what I need," exclaims Ronnie, her voice rising.

"Excuse me, just what *you* need?" This is not what I want to hear.

"I'm supposed to be home by now. Mom and Dad will be furious. They were pretty angry about Sunday night, so I'm trying to be a model daughter to make up for it. Not doing very well so far, am I?"

"Look, you go home, and I'll search for Moonlight," I say, hoping she won't take me up on it. After all, she's supposed to be my best friend, and best friends stick together, don't they?

Ronnie sounds relieved. "Really? Oh, you are a pal, Matty. Thanks. I'm sure he'll turn up. He can't be far," she says, hurrying away. "Anyway, Spike will be back later, so you won't be on your own for long." She is soon nothing more than a dot on the horizon, leaving me alone and abandoned. To say I am annoyed is putting it mildly.

I spend the next hour walking around the perimeter of the field, which is quite large, and discover that there is actually a gap in the fence where the wood has rotted and broken. It's certainly large enough for a horse to squeeze through. We should have checked more thoroughly.

Beyond the field is just wasteland, which some people use as a dumping ground for all sorts of trash, from grass cuttings to broken fridges and carpet remnants. That in turn backs onto two run-down housing developments, which are linked by a busy road. On the other side of the fort lies an abandoned railway track and more miles of wasteland with dips and gullies, which is accessed by a dirt track lined with hedges. Our horse could be anywhere.

I start walking again, aware that I have to find

Moonlight before it gets dark. Besides, I'm not looking forward to the idea of being alone in the fort at night. As I wander down the track toward the wasteland, I suddenly get the strangest feeling that I'm being watched. It's a horrible feeling, and makes the hairs on the back of my neck tingle. My mind begins to race. Who else, apart from my friends, knows that I'm here? My parents don't know. They think Moonlight is stabled at Miss Pugh's. If anything happens...

The light is fading and I imagine that I can hear footsteps. No, not footsteps, hoof beats. I'm being followed. I wish heartily that Spike had never told us the story of the Mad Major. The hoof beats sound nearer and nearer, and I start to run. But where do I run? I head back toward the old fort, running faster and faster, convinced I'm being pursued. What has happened to Spike? She should have been here by now. Now I'm reaching the fort, and strange thoughts are running through my mind. What if Moonlight isn't real? What if he is a ghost horse? After all, no one has claimed him. And now he's vanished into thin air, like he appeared out of thin air, and in a graveyard of all places. It's spooky.

I'm nearly out of breath now. The gate into the stable yard is closed. I remember now that Spike fixed it, and the catch is very stiff. I don't have time to fiddle with it, so I clamber over the gate and rush, panting, into the stable yard. Then I hear a horse whinny, and it's really close, maybe inches away. My heart misses a beat and then I see that Moonlight is standing in his stall, nonchalantly chewing a piece of hay.

"Moonlight?" I'm baffled, but before I can figure it out, a hand suddenly clamps onto my shoulder and I leap into the air and scream.

"Get a grip, Matty." The voice is familiar and I turn to come face to face with Spike.

"You idiot!" I yell. "You scared me half to death."

Seeing that I'm really frightened, Spike looks concerned.

"Hey, I didn't mean to upset you. Sorry I'm late. I had to help Dad with a repair job on the car. Goodness, Matty, you're as white as a ghost."

"So would you be if you had been chased by the Mad Major!"

"What are you talking about?"

"OK, so it might not have been a ghost. But someone – or something – is out there."

"Calm down, Matty. I just walked down the lane and I didn't see anyone."

"You mean you only just got here? So *you* didn't find Moonlight?"

"I didn't know he was missing. He was in the stable when I got here."

For a moment I laugh with relief. So Moonlight had been in his stable all the time. It was the obvious place to check, on reflection. It just didn't occur to me that he would have wandered back to his stable. "He was there all the time," I say to a puzzled Spike.

I start to tell her about Moonlight's disappearing act, and the gap in the fence, and Spike agrees to fix it in the morning. Then something strikes me.

"The gate into the yard. Was it shut when you arrived?" I ask.

Spike nods.

"And Moonlight was in his stable."

"Yes. Obviously you left the stable door open."

"That's right. We mucked out earlier and I was going to put some fresh shavings down."

"So?"

"And you're sure that the gate to the yard was closed?"

"Yes." Spike is getting impatient. "I've said so, haven't I? Don't you believe me?"

"I believe you. How high would you say that gate is? Six feet. More?"

"At least six feet," agrees Spike.

"And that gate is the only way into the yard?"

Spike nods. "What's your point?"

"How likely would you say it is that Moonlight can open and close the gate by himself?"

Spike laughs. "Not very."

"In that case, our horse can certainly jump! Maybe Moonlight *is* the reincarnation of the Mad Major's horse!"

Chapter 7

The next day, I test Moonlight's jumping ability. I decide against asking him to jump the six-foot gate (although I can see that Spike really likes the idea), and instead pop him over a fallen log on the ground. He pricks his ears forward and jumps it cheerfully several times. I'm pleased, and dismiss Gina's suggestion that someone unknown opened the gate last night. The thought of a stranger lurking at the fort is too creepy.

I ride back to my watching friends and announce, with a certain degree of self-satisfaction, "See, I said he can jump. He has great style. I'm going to enter him for the County Show and beat Mark and Snowstorm in the jumping contest."

The others think I'm asking for trouble, and that

I'm doomed to disappointment when Moonlight's owner turns up, but I begin training in earnest.

Spike helps me construct a jumping course from tires and oil drums and bits of wood gleaned from the dump. Ronnie cuts and ties together clumps of hedge from the lane to make a passable brush fence and Gina discovers an old trough that we fill with water to pass as a rather feeble water jump. Moonlight, however, manages to transcend his humble surroundings, and when he jumps the course clear each time everyone agrees that he looks every inch a champion.

"He jumps with feet to spare," declares Gina in admiration.

"He's a natural," agrees Ronnie.

"Maybe he is a reincarnation of the Mad Major's horse after all," laughs Spike, and I laugh too, but the joke makes me feel uneasy.

I begin to spend all my time at the fort with Moonlight (although I make sure I'm not there alone when it's dark). The others still try to divide their time between the stables and the fort, but with the County Show only a week away now, Spike and

Ronnie in particular need to practice at the stables. Spike is paying Miss Pugh to hire Soames for the jumping contest, and Ronnie's parents gave her the money to hire Everest (she had to pay more than she should, because lots of pupils wanted to borrow Everest, and Miss Pugh got them to "bid" for him, which I think is unethical). Poor Gina won't be able to enter any classes – her mother has made such a fuss about it that she doesn't want to upset her. Instead, Gina will be cheering us on.

I am a little miffed that, according to Ronnie, no one at the stables seems to miss me.

"Have you seen Snowstorm lately?" I ask.

"Maybe," replies Spike, mischievously.

"Yes, we have, and she's as gorgeous as ever, and jumping brilliantly," says Ronnie. "We're up against stiff competition for the jumping," admits Spike.

"Mark is a textbook rider," comments Gina.

"Yes, but don't you think his riding is a bit, well, unfeeling?" I add, dismounting from Moonlight and leading him back to the stable for a rubdown.

"What is this fascination with Mark?" teases Spike in a manner that I find irritating.

"What are you talking about, Spike? I have no interest in Mark whatsoever. I don't know why you think otherwise."

"Touched a nerve, there, didn't I?" giggles Spike, running off before I can hit her. To my annoyance I find I'm blushing.

Later, Ronnie takes me aside and says, "You shouldn't get at Spike like this. I know she can be a bit of a pain sometimes, but she is paying the lion's share of Moonlight's upkeep."

It was true. Since we all failed miserably to get part time jobs, we are all chipping in with pocket money to pay for food for Moonlight, and Spike is contributing more than any of us. This is because her parents give her a bigger allowance than the rest of us (which, as she rightly points out, she has to work for) but to be fair she never makes a big thing out of the fact that she's supporting the horse that I get to ride more than anyone else. I resolve to apologize to her.

"Anyway," continues Ronnie, "If you really are going to ride Moonlight in the Show, we have to find you a saddle. I doubt if the rules will allow you to enter riding bareback."

"You're right," I agree. "Do you think any of Miss

Pugh's horses are about the same size as Moonlight? If so, we could borrow a saddle."

"Not ideal. Anyway, most of the horses are being used for the Show."

I consider this. "But we can't possibly afford to buy a saddle."

"It's a problem, isn't it?" and Ronnie frowns.

We all sit outside and eat burgers and fries for lunch. Spike came across a burger joint near the housing development a couple of days ago, and we've been eager to try it out. The food is a bit greasy, but we're all hungry and it makes a change from our usual sandwiches.

We drink cans of soda (with the exception of Gina, who is heavily into mineral water and warns us of the dangers of artificial additives), and laugh and joke together, and I feel lucky to have such great friends. Then they all return to Miss Pugh's, leaving me with the radio for company. For a while I just sit and gaze into space, imagining myself riding to victory in the County Show, and smile at the look of surprise that I'm sure will be on Mark's face when I beat him. Then I realize that the clock is ticking, and I need to tidy up the yard before taking Moonlight out for a ride.

It's warm and sunny again, so I wrap my shirt around the radio and hide it in the stable (just in case we do get a mystery visitor), then ride out on Moonlight in my T-shirt and bike shorts.

Although our surroundings aren't particularly attractive, it's pleasant to daydream as Moonlight walks and jogs. I'm reflecting on what a trustworthy horse he is when he suddenly stops and tenses. His ears are alert and he gives a short whinny. To my surprise, there's a distant answering whinny followed by a feeble, "Hello?" and I wonder if someone is in trouble. I haven't encountered any other riders out here before, and Spike won't bring any riders out near the fort in case people see Moonlight. We like the idea of keeping him secret – and I, for one, have no wish for my parents to find out that he's not being kept at Miss Pugh's. They would not be at all eager to have us hanging out in this area.

"Come on, Moonlight, find the pony," I say, feeling like a heroine in a horsy adventure.

He trots on enthusiastically and within minutes we encounter a familiar white pony.

"Snowstorm!" I exclaim. She's standing with her reins dangling, and although her rider isn't entirely visible, I can make out a leg and a flailing arm from her other side.

I dismount, keeping a tight hold of Moonlight and approach Snowstorm quietly, saying, "Easy, girl," in soothing tones until I can grab hold of her reins.

"Thank goodness," says Mark sheepishly. I peer down to see him lying in an undignified position with his foot caught in the stirrup. His face is dirty, and his usually pristine jodhpurs grass-stained. He looks pretty silly, and I try not to giggle.

"What happened?" I ask, attempting to free his foot.

"One minute we were trotting by the abandoned railway track, the next she just took off," he starts to explain. "Something scared her, but I don't know what. I couldn't see anything. Then she stumbled and I fell, but my foot got jammed in the stirrup."

"The ground is very uneven around here," I remark. "I would never ride fast along here in case my horse hurts his legs." It ends up sounding as if I'm telling him off, so I add, "It was bad luck to get your foot stuck." I push harder on his boot and, as I've forgotten to support his leg as it becomes free, it bangs on the ground.

"Oops, sorry. Did that hurt?"

Mark shakes his head, but he rubs his foot anyway. "No, it's my arm that hurts. I hit it hard when I landed. It's painful to move, which is why I couldn't reach up and free myself."

"Is it broken?" I ask, suddenly concerned.

"No, just bruised." He brushes himself down with his good hand. "Thanks. I'm glad you came along when you did."

For a moment our eyes meet and I notice how clear and sad his eyes are. My stomach does a little leap.

"We'd better make sure that Snowstorm is OK," I say hastily and I check her legs for heat or swelling, but she seems fine.

"Can you get back on?" I ask.

He nods, but adds, "I'd like to sit down for while first. Get my breath back."

"OK," I say, preparing to remount Moonlight and leave him to it. I have done my Good Samaritan bit.

"He's a nice looking horse," says Mark abruptly, gesturing to Moonlight.

"Yes, he is," I agree proudly.

An awkward silence follows, so I fill it with, "Do you often ride out here? Not many people do, you know."

"I've been past the old fort a few times," he replies and it almost sounds like an admission of guilt. A thought strikes me.

"When?" I ask.

He shrugs. "Now and then."

"Ever ride out here at night?"

"I might have."

"When?" I repeat.

"Only once – a week ago. Hey, this sounds like an inquisition."

"So it could have been *you* that night, scaring me to death! I thought it was the Mad Major!"

Mark looks bewildered, so I tell him the legend of the Mad Major, and when he can see that I was quite scared that night, he looks sheepish again, and admits that he knows about the old fort and our keeping Moonlight there, because he followed us once.

At first I'm furious. "You followed us? How *dare* you!" and I rant for a bit until he seems suitably contrite.

"I'm sorry," he says quietly. "I didn't mean to scare anyone. I was just curious. You all seem to have such fun together." He stops abruptly and I sense the envy in his tone and realize from what I've seen myself, and from what the others have said, that Mark is always alone at the stables. He never talks to anyone, nor does he seem to have friends there. I wonder if he's lonely.

"I think I should be getting back now," he announces, blushing, as if he has said more than he intended.

"Will you be all right?" I take a deep breath and add, "Would you like me to ride back with you?"

He looks grateful for a second, then recovers his usual controlled composure and says, "If it doesn't take you out of your way, maybe you would ride with me down the track to the road." I lead Snowstorm to a little hilly bit of ground, which Mark can use as a mounting block, and we ride side by side.

"Why were you so rude to me that day at the stables?" he asks suddenly and I am taken aback. "You know, when everyone was out on the trail ride and I found you talking to Snowstorm as if she was another friend."

"I don't remember," I reply vaguely, not wanting to.

"Why don't you like me?"

I swallow hard. Now *I'm* the one being questioned, and I don't like it.

"It's not you, Mark. After all, I hardly know you. It's just that, well, I was jealous of you."

"Jealous of me? Why on earth would you be jealous of me?" He sounds genuinely puzzled.

"Snowstorm. You've got Snowstorm, and she's wonderful, and I've always wanted a pony like that."

"Oh." He considers this. "But you have a horse, too."

"You mean Moonlight? Well, to be honest he doesn't actually belong to me, although I like to think he does. Well, not yet, anyway, but I hope..." And then I end up telling him all about Moonlight, how we found him in the graveyard, how no one has claimed him, and then my hopes for the show. At this point I stop. I've said too much.

"You have an interesting life," says Mark enviously.

I laugh. "I never thought of it like that."

I realize that we've ridden well beyond the road, and in fact are not that far from my house. I've been talking so much that the time has just flown.

"Does your arm still hurt?" I ask.

He nods and winces.

"Oh, dear, I hope your arm will be alright for the

show," I say. Of course, if he is out of the proceedings then Moonlight and I have a really good chance of winning. I feel guilty for having such an ungenerous thought so to make up for it I say, "We're not far from my house and I'm really thirsty, so would you like to come back for a drink?"

He replies, "Yes" almost before I have finished the sentence. I begin to wonder what Mark will think of my home and parents. He clearly comes from money. You can hear it in the way he speaks and dresses. He seems so self-assured, although I'm aware that I've started to see another side of him. I look across at him, sitting so perfectly on his perfect pony. He is actually smiling a little.

Why should I worry? I tell myself. Why should I want to impress him? He's just a guy, after all.

As we reach my house I whisper hastily, "Don't mention the old fort to my parents. They think we keep Moonlight at Miss Pugh's."

"I won't tell," he replies, enjoying the subterfuge.

We dismount and I push open the garden gate. It's early evening by now, so both my parents will be home from work. They're sitting in the garden, sunning themselves.

Dad looks up from his deck chair. "Hi, Matty."

Then, to my amazement, he smiles at Mark as if he's an old pal and adds, "Oh, hello, Mark. This is a nice surprise. I didn't know you're a friend of Matty's."

Chapter 8

I'm amazed. "You know each other?"

Dad nods and smiles. "Mark plays in the jazz band. A darned fine clarinetist he is, too."

I try, without success, to stop my mouth from dropping open in amazement.

"Matty, Hon, are you going to stand there all day holding those ponies?" says Mom, and I can tell by the way she's studying Mark that she's quite curious about him.

I loosen Snowstorm's girth and tether her and Moonlight by the garden shed.

"I didn't know you played a musical instrument," I say to Mark.

He shrugs, as if it's nothing.

"Would you like to stay for dinner, Mark?" Mom

asks and before I can get a word in he says, "Yes, please, Mrs. Matthews, that would be very nice."

"Why don't you come and give me a hand, Matty?" suggests Mom, and I can tell it's an order rather than an invitation. So I follow her into the kitchen, leaving Mark and Dad to chat together.

"Who is that nice young man?" Mom demands to know in a hushed tone that I am convinced Mark can hear through the open door.

"Mom, please," I groan.

"Well, you've never brought a boy home before, Matty. He's very polite."

"I hardly know him, and I've only brought him home because he fell off his pony and hurt his arm and I decided to help him out. That's all there is to it."

"All right, Matty, if you say so," she says with a knowing smile. Honestly, she's as bad as Spike.

Thankfully, dinner is ready soon, and I help carry it out into the back yard. Everyone chats politely, and I hope I don't look too embarrassed. Then Snowstorm starts to paw the grass impatiently so I decide to go and make a fuss over her before Dad gets overprotective about his lawn. Mark follows me.

"Does your arm still hurt?" I ask, wishing I could think of something more intelligent to say.

"It does a bit," he replies. "But I'm sure it's just a bruise."

Another silence follows.

"Your parents are nice people," he says.

I nod. "Yes. I moan about them, but I'm lucky really. At least they don't try to control me like Gina's mother does. Poor Gina."

"She's one of your friends at the stables, isn't she? The pretty one with blonde hair."

"Yes, that's Gina," I reply, my tone sounding more clipped than I intend.

"I wish my Dad was more like yours," Mark says wistfully.

"Don't you get along with your Dad?" I ask.

"On and off."

"He seems pretty strict."

"He can be demanding."

"You're not scared of him, are you?" and as soon as the words are out, I regret them.

"Of course not!" Mark's tone is prickly. "What makes you think that?"

"Oh, I didn't mean ... I'm sorry. I shouldn't have –"

"Dad is a successful businessman. He sets very high standards, and I can't always live up to them," Mark says sadly. "That disappoints both of us."

We make a fuss over Snowstorm, and then Moonlight, so he doesn't get jealous, though I must say that he is such a laid back sort of horse, I don't imagine Moonlight getting worked up about anything. Snowstorm brushes her lips on my hair and gives a soft whinny. I look into her liquid eyes and my heart melts.

"You're so lucky to have such a terrific pony," I sigh.

"I know," agrees Mark. "And she's wasted on me. I don't deserve her." Then he drops another bombshell. "You see, I don't really like riding."

"What? You don't like riding?" I'm puzzled. "Then why do you ride?"

"To please my Dad," says Mark. He explains, "My brother Joe was a far better rider than I am, destined to be a champion, if things had worked out. But he was killed in a car crash a year ago. Seems like yesterday in some ways. Dad always liked him best. No use pretending otherwise." He looks so sad that for a moment (only a moment, mind you), I want to give him a hug.

But I restrain myself and he continues, "So I tried to step into Joe's shoes, tried to replace him. But I couldn't get along with his horse, Clipper, a highly strung thoroughbred. So we sold Clipper and Dad bought Snowstorm. Then Mom left us, and everything seemed to fall apart, so we moved here, to make a fresh start."

"Poor Mark." I don't know what else to say. He must have had a miserable time. No wonder he still seems so unhappy. He could do with a friend.

Suddenly he smiles. "I'd much rather be a jazz musician than a show jumper, you know."

"Then why don't you tell your father that?" I hear myself saying.

By now, Mark thinks it's time to get back home, so he thanks my parents for dinner and gets ready to go. I offer him an upturned bucket to make a mounting block and hold Snowstorm while he gets on. He winces, and I can see that his arm still hurts.

"Will you be all right on your own? Would you like me to come back with you, just in case?" I offer.

"Would you mind, Matty?" he replies gratefully. "Sorry to inconvenience you and all that, but I would appreciate it."

So we set off down the road and head for Mark's house, which he says is only a couple of miles away.

"Our horses seem to get on well together," he remarks, and I add, "just as well, really."

"Dad seems to have high hopes for Snowstorm's chances at the Show," says Mark. "He has his heart set on the jumping trophy."

I grin. "So do I. But my biggest problem at the moment is where to get a saddle. I can't ride Moonlight bareback in the jumping contest."

"It would cause quite a stir," Mark agrees. "But it would be fun." He looks pensive for a while and then says, "I know. We still have Clipper's saddle. Dad will never admit it, but he got sentimental after we sold Clipper, so he hung onto the saddle. I think he just wanted to keep something of Joe's. Anyway, we could try it on Moonlight, and if it fits, you can borrow it for the Show!"

I am taken aback by his generosity. "Are you sure? It's very kind of you, but –"

"It's the least I can do. If you hadn't come along when you did, I don't know what would have happened."

"Oh, come off it, Snowstorm wouldn't have gone anywhere," I say casually.

"Don't argue. I insist."

Mark's house is everything I imagined – large, modern, in a brand-new housing development on the outskirts of town with Georgian coach lamps outside the front door and a long gravel drive framed by perfectly manicured lawns. A horse trailer is parked to one side.

"When Dad gets back from work, I'll get him to take Snowstorm back to Miss Pugh's in the horse trailer," says Mark as we put Moonlight and Snowstorm in the large enclosed back yard. Peering at Moonlight he suddenly says, "You know, Moonlight does seem kind of familiar, somehow. I can't think why, though."

"Funny, that's what Gina keeps saying," I reply.

He lets himself in with a key, glances briefly at a note left on the kitchen table by their cleaning lady, Anthea, and offers me some lemonade. While I'm drinking it, he disappears upstairs.

I study my surroundings. The big sunny lounge is carefully and tastefully furnished, and immaculately clean and tidy. I reflect that Mom would love to have an Anthea to clean for her. Then I become aware of how empty the house feels; sort of lonely. No homey atmosphere.

While I'm reflecting on this, Mark reappears with Clipper's saddle. It smells like new leather.

"Let's try it on Moonlight, shall we?" he suggests.

Moonlight regards the saddle with mild interest and sniffs at it before we put it on. To my delight, it could have been made for him. Even if it's not quite a perfect fit, it's close enough. I grin like an idiot.

Mark smiles. "Now we're even."

"But won't your Dad mind?"

"Not if I don't tell him."

I'm about to thank him when a thought crosses my mind. "Mark, how did you manage to carry that heavy saddle with your bruised arm. Has it stopped hurting already?"

"Oh, that." He looks sheepish. "Well, I have to be honest with you. It stopped hurting hours ago."

I am indignant. "But why didn't you –"

"I like your company. I wanted you to ride back with me. Is that so terrible?"

"You tricked me!" I don't know whether to be angry or amused.

"So," Mark says playfully. "Still think you're going to beat me in the jumping contest?"

"You bet I'll beat you! And how!" I exclaim.

Chapter 9

I've dreamed of this day for so long now that I can hardly believe it's happening. Any minute I expect something to go wrong – Moonlight to go lame, or the police to appear and say he has been claimed, or Mark's father demanding the return of Clipper's saddle, or ... Well, there are a host of things that can go wrong, aren't there?

"Be positive," advises Ronnie, proudly displaying the blue rosette she has just won with Everest in the Showing Class. "Just live for the moment."

So that is what I'm trying to do, as I prepare to go into the ring.

"Here we are, at the County Show," I tell Moonlight, as he canters into the ring at a nice collected pace. I have to concentrate really hard, because part of my mind keeps wandering. The last week seems to have whizzed by. The others were delighted when I told them about Mark lending me the saddle in return for rescuing him, and Spike gave me a knowing smile, but I didn't tell them of my long conversation with Mark, and the problems with his father. I felt that he had talked to me in confidence and I didn't want to spoil his trust. Even so, my friends knew that something must have happened, because I stopped making critical comments about Mark and spoke about him in much more friendly terms. I did, however, admit to Ronnie (who is sworn to secrecy) that Mark has phoned me every day this week.

Soames and Spike have already jumped. They got four faults after Spike turned Soames too sharply at the approach to the wall and he jumped too soon and knocked a brick off. I'm determined not to make the same mistake.

Moonlight clears the first three jumps easily, his ears pricked forward, full of enthusiasm. I try not to interfere too much – he seems to know exactly what to do. Then we turn for the wall, more cautiously than Spike, and Moonlight stays balanced so he approaches slowly but carefully. We jump clear, and then take the double, and the gate, and the funny brush fence with garishly painted poles, which has spooked several of the previous horses. But Moonlight soars over, with the air of a horse who knows his job so thoroughly that he could do it in his sleep.

We complete a perfect round to the sound of cheers and applause. I'll never forget it. I pat Moonlight's neck and rub his mane, and feel a little twinge of emotion. I really love this horse.

"What a great round!" shouts Ronnie, who is waiting at the ringside. "How can anyone beat that? Even Mark and Snowstorm couldn't do better."

I'm still grinning stupidly when I notice Mark nearby, ready to go next. I hope he hasn't heard.

I say, "Good luck," but his face is set in a grim line and I wonder if he noticed me. Gina offers to take Moonlight and cool him down so I can watch Mark. At least that way she gets to ride for a bit. It must be very frustrating for her, not being able to take part when I know she would love to. But she doesn't want to take the risk of someone seeing her and it getting back to her mother, who would go bananas, and then Gina would be banned from riding altogether.

It feels strange watching Mark, knowing that he

doesn't like riding. I see him differently now, and I wonder if anyone else can tell how he feels by watching him ride. What makes a good rider? Is it merely a matter of technique? Mark certainly has that, and compared to me he has oodles of style, but what about having a natural affinity for the horse? Surely that is vital, and he lacks that; he says so himself. Some people connect with animals, and some don't. Maybe, in the end, that matters more than technique and ability.

Snowstorm is on form, jumping faultlessly, and I'm hardly surprised, despite Ronnie's comments, that Mark and Snowstorm go clear.

Out of the ten remaining riders, only one other, a freckle-faced guy on a deceptively agile cob, gets a clear round, so there will be three of us in the jump-off.

I have to stop myself from trembling as the jumps are raised.

"You can do it," says Spike with conviction.

"Yes, show them what you can do," adds Ronnie.

Gina gives one of her reassuring smiles, and I'm touched by my friends' support.

Moonlight yawns, wondering what all the fuss is

about, and then we're cantering into the ring and, before I realize it, already up and over the first jump.

"Focus," I tell myself fiercely.

We clear the second and the third and then we approach the wall, and suddenly it looks enormous, much higher than I would have imagined.

"Moonlight can do it," I tell myself. "After all, he cleared that huge gate at the fort – well, we think he did." And this split second of self doubt must have communicated itself to Moonlight, because he falters slightly at the approach, and I have to urge him on with my legs. But by then, it's too late to correct the hesitation and he just clips the top row of bricks with his forelegs and I hear a brick crashing to the ground.

I berate myself, knowing it's my fault, but I work even harder for the remainder of the round and we emerge with a respectable four faults.

"Bad luck," says Mark in commiseration as we pass on my way out of the ring.

I smile feebly, annoyed at myself for losing faith in Moonlight. If I had put my trust in him we would have gone clear.

"Never mind," says Gina. "You might still win."

We all watch Mark. Twice, Snowstorm brushes a

pole with her hind legs, and twice we expect the rattling pole to fall, but she's lucky, and with a final effort at the last jump, they finish with a clear round.

I feel a mixture of emotions; pleased with Mark's success, knowing what it means to his father, but frustrated at losing my chance of winning, and envious that it was Mark, and not I, riding Snowstorm.

"It's not over yet," says Spike. "There's still one more rider."

The boy on the cob looks full of confidence, and as he clears each jump with great aplomb, it seems as if Mark will be accepting a blue rosette after all. And then, at the last jump, the cob falls victim to the garish poles. I recall that he wasn't too crazy about this jump the first time around, and that the boy had given him an extra kick to clear it. This time, however, the cob stares at the offending obstacle with growing suspicion, his steps slowing inexorably as it looms ever nearer. He skids to a definitive halt.

"Three faults," breathes Spike.

"That puts you in third place, Matty," adds Gina, as if I don't realize that.

The boy approaches the jump again, with a look of great determination and for a moment I think that the cob will jump, but at the last minute he loses confidence and refuses. The boy sighs, circles and gives the cob a good talking to and at the third attempt he clears the jump and they finish with six faults.

"Second place, Matty!" shrieks Gina with delight, and before I know it we're riding into the ring to collect our blue rosette and modest cash prize. So I haven't beaten Mark after all. I feel disappointed, but more because I think I've let Moonlight down than anything else.

As we complete our lap of victory, I notice a familiar figure waving from the front row.

"Dad? Shouldn't you be playing golf today?"

He grins and waves. "Took time out to see my daughter. Well done! See you later!"

I wave back, pleased that he's come to support me. As Mark and I ride out of the ring I see Mark's father rushing towards us. I panic. Maybe he'll demand the immediate return of Clipper's saddle. Still, at least I had it when I needed it, although it'll be odd going back to bareback riding again. But instead he says, "Well done, both of you. Good riding. I'm glad to see that Joe's saddle has been put to good use. I'm proud of you, Mark."

I'm flabbergasted, and I must admit that Mark seems a little surprised.

For some reason, I'm struck dumb, particularly when Mark's father tells me I can hang on to the saddle for as long as I need it. I manage to burble, "Thank you," before he takes off for the refreshment tent. I wonder if he realizes that I'm the same girl who rode his son's pony without permission, and who he told to stay away from Snowstorm, or else. It does seem like a long time ago now.

"Let me buy you an ice cream cone," offers Mark.

We dismount and lead our worthy steeds behind us while we walk to the ice cream truck. "I've been doing some thinking," begins Mark seriously, "and I've decided to take your advice."

I feel a bit nervous, wondering what he's going to say next. Then Mark reveals that he finally told his father that he wants to be a jazz musician and not a rider.

"How did he react?" I demand to know.

"Badly, at first," Mark admits. "But then we had a long heart-to-heart talk. Eventually, after a lot of discussion, he agreed with me. And he's also accepted that I want to give up riding."

"That's great," I respond. An uncomfortable thought strikes me. If Mark gives up riding, what will happen to Snowstorm? I voice my concerns.

"That's the hard part," admits Mark. "I've actually grown very fond of her, in a way, but she's wasted on me. So..."

I try to complete the sentence I long to hear: "So I've decided to give her to you." My heart starts to thump and I tremble with anticipation.

But instead Mark says, "So I've decided to sell Snowstorm. In fact we've already had an offer, earlier today."

"Oh." This is not what I want to hear. Suddenly things don't look so great. I sense that a cloud is gathering.

Mark adds hastily, "She'll go to a great home; very knowledgeable, and very horsy. You would approve."

I still have a faint glimmer of hope. Perhaps Mark is about to tell me that my parents have bought Snowstorm, as a surprise.

"Where does this possible new owner live?" I ask, trying to sound casual.

"In the next County. They're a show jumping family."

"Oh."

So I'm going to lose Snowstorm after all. And it's entirely my fault. If I hadn't tried to persuade Mark to stand up to his father and say what he really wanted, this would probably never have happened. Oh, the irony of it.

"So, what flavor would you like? Vanilla or strawberry?" asks Mark as we reach the ice cream truck.

"Both," I reply grimly. "With masses of chocolate sprinkles on top, and lots of whipped cream." I need sugar to help me get over the shock.

Mark pulls a face but orders it anyway. I'm just about to take a great big lick when I notice two uniformed policemen walking toward us purposefully. To my consternation the tallest policeman looks at me sternly and says, "We have reason to believe that you are in possession of a stolen horse."

Chapter 10

The next ten minutes are a living nightmare.

Mark establishes with the policemen that they have had an anonymous call from someone at the show who has recognized Moonlight and says he has been stolen, so they are bound to investigate. One of them tries to grab Moonlight's reins and take him away, by which time I am shouting and getting increasingly upset, and the ensuing commotion has attracted quite a crowd. Gina and Spike appear, and then, while I'm fighting with the policeman who wants to take Moonlight, Ronnie comes running over with my father.

She puts her arm around me and tries to calm me down while my father talks at length with the policemen. Finally, the police leave and Dad explains he's given them our name and address, explained that we *had* reported the horse missing, and agreed to go to the police station to sort things out.

"In the meantime, we can hang onto Moonlight. I suggest we take him back to Miss Pugh's stables for the time being. I'll come back with you and make her aware of the situation."

At this stage, I realize we have to tell the truth about where we are actually keeping Moonlight. When he discovers I've been lying to him, Dad is furious.

Mark tries to intervene on my behalf, and argue our case, but I don't think Dad is really listening. In the end, Dad takes me home and the others are entrusted to return Moonlight to the fort until we await the outcome from the police investigation. It's all a big mess.

Mom is more sympathetic, but she can understand Dad's annoyance. Waiting for him to return from the police station is unbearable, and he has refused to let me go with him. At six thirty, Mom starts to make sandwiches, but I'm not hungry. By now Gina, Spike, Ronnie and Mark have all returned from the fort, anxious for any news.

Earlier on, the police had said something about our horse being a TV star, and that he was used for a commercial for mints.

"Surely he's not the horse that used to be in the commercial for Moonlight Mints?" wonders Gina. "You know, where he leaps over mountains and streams so that his rider can bring mint chocolates to the woman of his dreams."

"I don't remember seeing that," I respond. "You have a vivid imagination, Gina."

Gina looks hurt, and Ronnie says, "I have a vague memory of that. A long time ago."

"Now that you mention it, I remember a commercial for Moonlight Mints with a horse in it," my Mom chimes in. "That was a few years ago, though. They use a sports car now."

"That was the last one. They use computer animation in the latest one, with morphing techniques," begins Spike, at which point I shout, "Oh, be quiet!"

"There's no need to be rude, Matty. We're all worried," Gina admonishes me.

Then Mark says, "I don't know about this commercial, but when I saw Moonlight in action today, he did remind me of a horse that used to be ridden by that show jumper who had to retire after he had a bad fall. His jumping style is so similar." He looks pensive. "I thought before that Moonlight looked familiar."

I'm getting fed up with everyone turning into Sherlock Holmes all of a sudden. But before an argument can ensue, Dad arrives home.

"Thank goodness," breathes Mom.

We all shout at once, until Dad looks stern, at which point we become silent and listen to what he has to tell us.

"First, as upsetting as this will be for all of you, I have to report that Moonlight does have an owner. I'm afraid you won't be able to keep him."

I start to feel sick. First I lost Snowstorm, and now Moonlight, and all in the space of a day.

Dad tries to explain to us that Moonlight is in fact Socrates, an ex-show jumper (which explains why he's such a great jumper) who retired and was then used in television commercials some years ago. So it seems that Gina and Mark were both right. Socrates was very valuable for a while and was bought by an entrepreneurial businessman as an investment. But when he was no longer used for the commercials, he lost value, and the owner, who had him insured for a considerable sum of money at the height of his fame, decided to "lose" the horse deliberately as part of an insurance fraud. I don't quite understand the details, although Ronnie and Mark seem to, but the owner had no desire to recover Socrates, since he had now claimed the insurance money. He had paid some of his shady acquaintances to "steal" the horse and take him to the other side of the country, but they had a minor accident while transporting him. Socrates escaped from the horse trailer and traveled alone until he ended up in the graveyard, where we found him. It all sounded very complicated and elaborate.

"So, if the owner doesn't want him back, why can't we keep Moonlight?" I ask.

"Socrates," corrects Gina.

"I'm afraid it isn't that simple," says my Dad. "His owner is already facing criminal charges for other shady deals, and is more than likely facing a jail sentence for the more serious charges. While he's away, his niece is handling his affairs, and she wants Socrates back."

"It isn't fair!" I exclaim. "They treat a horse as if he's just a piece of property, or a business investment, and then expect to just turn up and take him away again. They don't deserve to have a horse."

"We don't know that his niece is like that," remarks my Mom, which is really irritating.

"Of course she is! They're obviously criminals, the bunch of them."

"Anyway, we don't know for sure that Moonlight is Socrates," exclaims Spike, trying to save the situation. "There has been no official identification, has there?"

My father nods. "You're right. Which is why the niece, Carly Bridges, will be phoning us shortly to arrange to look at the horse. She does have proof of ownership, but, as you say, it might not be her horse."

This is the thought I cling to when I try, without success, to sleep that night.

When I awaken the next morning, with a splitting headache, Ms. Bridges has already phoned and my parents have arranged for her to see Moonlight just before lunch.

"It'll be more convenient for everyone if she sees the horse here," Dad tells me over his coffee. I know he doesn't want her to see Moonlight at the old fort. "So would you go and get the horse after breakfast, to allow plenty of time?"

"And, please, Matty, don't go doing some disappearing act with Moonlight," pleads my Mom. "It'll only lead to more trouble, and we've got enough of that already."

As if I would!

On my way out, Ronnie arrives and we walk down the road together, with heavy hearts. She goes to get Gina and Spike (in that order, so Gina's mother won't know Spike is with us) while I go on to the old fort so I'll have some time alone with Moonlight.

He whinnies a greeting as usual at my approach and senses that I'm troubled, which I find really touching. As I give him a cuddle I say, "You aren't Socrates, are you? Promise me you're not."

I take him out in the field for what I pray will not be the last time, and we have a great canter, and then jump Spike's homemade course. Then the others arrive, and we agree to take turns riding Moonlight back to my house.

"Don't worry, I'm sure things will work out," says Spike trying to sound cheerful.

We have lots of time to spare, so we stop at the corner shop and the others buy me a huge ice cream to make up for the one I never got to eat at the show, which is very sweet of them.

I'm the last to ride Moonlight, and when we draw up to the house I notice an unfamiliar car parked outside, and a horse trailer.

"It's too early," I protest. "She said just before lunch. It's only just eleven."

"Some people have lunch early," says Gina, unhelpfully.

"She must be pretty confident it's Socrates, to have brought the horse trailer," observes Spike.

"Not necessarily," says Ronnie. "She may have brought it just in case."

I wish they would be quiet. Already, I hate Carly Bridges.

With trepidation, I tether Moonlight in the back yard and go inside. An attractive young woman with short honey-blonde hair, blue eyes and a friendly smile sits at the table with my parents, sipping tea.

"You must be Matty," she says politely.

I stare rudely. She is wearing black leggings, jodhpur boots and a baggy white T-shirt, and when she stands up I can see that she is infuriatingly slim.

"Well, I think we ought to take a look at the horse," says Dad, anxious to get it over with.

What happens next takes us all by surprise. As

soon as Carly Bridges steps outside, Moonlight gives a shrill whinny of recognition and shakes his head excitedly.

"My baby!" exclaims Carly and she throws her arms around the horse's neck and buries her face in his black mane. He nuzzles her hair and she sobs a bit while we watch, feeling embarrassed and awkward. Then she turns, her face tear-stained.

"I can't thank you enough for finding him," she beams, grabbing my hand and squeezing it. "My uncle told me he had been stolen and had probably been taken out of state. I thought I would never see him again."

"That's OK," I mutter lamely. I know for certain that all my hopes of hanging on to Moonlight are well and truly dashed.

After this emotional reunion we know that the checking of the relevant paperwork is almost a formality. I hate to admit it, but it's obvious to everyone that Carly and Moonlight are meant to be together. And she turns out to be a nice person. She thanks everyone again, and then Moonlight is loaded into the horse trailer. I say a tearful goodbye, and kiss him, before rushing to my room to have a good cry while he's driven away. I can't bear to watch him go.

Two days later I have to go through it all over again when Snowstorm is sold. At least Mark lets me have a farewell ride on her before she's taken off. I won't go into detail (it's too upsetting); suffice to say that I have a wonderful ride on Snowstorm, a taste of what might have been, before I say goodbye to her. Before I leave, Mark asks me if I'll go to the movies with him on Saturday, and I say yes.

So here we are. Back to square one. No Moonlight. No Snowstorm. Hanging out at Miss Pugh's stables. We are once again the pony-less club, thinking of ways to raise money to buy our pony before Christmas. Sad, isn't it?

As the week goes on, I try to adjust to normality, but it isn't easy. I miss going to the old fort to be with Moonlight. I wonder how Snowstorm is getting on in her new home. Mom and Dad are being great. They know how important Moonlight was to me, so they haven't belabored the fact that I lied to them about keeping Moonlight at Miss Pugh's.

Anyway, it's Saturday afternoon, and Gina, Spike,

Ronnie and I are sitting in the tack room at the stables, washing bits and cleaning bridles, and my mind is wandering to what I'll wear when I meet Mark at the movies tonight, when Miss Pugh comes in and makes an announcement.

"Thank you, girls, for your help over the years, but it will no longer be needed." She's grinning broadly.

We exchange puzzled glances.

She continues, "I've finally given in to Eric, and I've agreed to marry him."

"Congratulations," say Ronnie and Gina in unison.

"Who is Eric?" whispers Spike. Miss Pugh obviously hears because she says, "Eric Brinton, the owner of the car lot."

"Oh." I try to imagine this. I've seen Eric on a number of occasions, and the two of them together seems like a strange union. I wonder why Miss Pugh's marriage should affect us.

"Eric is eager for me to go into business with him," explains Miss Pugh. "So I've sold the stables and land to him, to expand his car lot, and I'll take over all the paperwork while he concentrates on selling cars. Of course, you're all invited to the wedding." With that, she practically skips off, grinning wildly. We stare at each other, dumbfounded, while the full significance of what she's just said sinks in.

"You know what this means?" I say in horror. "The stables will cease to be. All the horses will be sold. Our last pony haven has been taken from us. We will truly be pony-less."

Chapter 11

Have you ever found yourself in a situation where you think it can't possibly get any worse – and then it does? Well, you'll know exactly how I feel, then.

I'm sitting on the bus, on my way to the movies to meet Mark. Normally I would have been looking forward to this, having spent ages deciding what to wear. But everything feels flat. In the end I threw on a kind of dull beige cotton dress with capped sleeves that I know does nothing for me, and I'm finding it hard to get up any enthusiasm.

As the bus pulls up, five minutes late, there's no sign of Mark, and I wonder if he's had second thoughts. Maybe he won't turn up after all. And then I walk into the foyer, and there he is, flicking through a free film magazine that details coming attractions.

"Hi, you look nice," he says, and I think he needs to have his eyes tested, but I smile and say, "So do you," and he laughs. We join the line for the film, which is billed as a zany comedy. It will probably do me good, but I'm not in the mood. Mark keeps looking at me, and it must be so obvious that I'm fed up that he says, "Is a date with me that bad? I mean, you didn't have to come out tonight."

I realize he's serious, so I hasten to reassure him that it has nothing to do with him.

"So why so gloomy?" he persists, and once again I find myself talking to him like I've known him for years, and he hears about Miss Pugh and the impending closure of the stables.

"Look, I can see that you don't really want to see this movie, so why don't we just go for a burger and soda?" he suggests.

We do, and have a nice time, under the circumstances. I realize that Mark has already become a good friend.

I'm surprised when he doesn't get in touch at all the

following week, but still preoccupied with the stables to make too much of it. Miss Pugh has wasted no time, and there's already a sign on the gate saying "Sold for Development." I've noticed that Eric is spending a lot of time at the stables (which is now referred to as *The Site*) with a team of workmen. It's all so sad, and I'm having nightmares, worrying about what will happen to our beloved horses and ponies. The future looks pony-less.

Then, one morning, Mark turns up at my house really early. In fact, I've just gotten up, my hair is all over the place, and my eyes are bleary.

"Hurry up and get ready. We're going for a walk," he says excitedly.

So I drag a brush through my hair while he waits in the yard, and we set off purposefully. At first, Mark won't tell me where we're going. Then I realize that we're heading for the old fort. I haven't been there since Moonlight left, so I have mixed emotions when I see it again. I wonder what Mark is up to.

"Look," he says, gesturing to the derelict buildings and the acres and acres of wasteland. "What do you see?"

"A mess," I retort.

"You're wrong," he replies, grabbing my hand and squeezing it hard. "I see stables, horses, people –"

"Then you're nuts," I reply, turning to go.

"Look again," he urges. I do, and Mark continues, "This land is ripe for development, and my father was looking for a new project, so he bought it."

I'm disappointed in Mark, to say the least. "Why? To build yet another supermarket or industrial park?"

He shakes his head. "No. A riding school."

"Sorry. I don't think I heard you right."

"Dad is going to make this into a riding school – or, rather, an equestrian center. He thinks the old fort would make a really unusual setting for a riding center, it's so full of atmosphere, and he'll try to keep the character of the original buildings. There's so much land here that he could really expand; build an indoor school, a jumping arena, a cross-country course ..."

"Hang on, Mark. Did you say *your Dad*? But does he know anything about horses?"

Mark laughs. "He taught Joe everything he knew. He's a terrific teacher. A bit strict, though. He's really excited about the project. It will be a sort of memorial to Joe."

He grins. "That's why I haven't been in touch. I wanted to wait until I knew for sure. It's something Dad started to talk about after the County Show, but when you told me about Miss Pugh selling, that was the final encouragement he needed. So you don't need to worry about Miss Pugh's horses. Dad has bought them all, with the tack, equipment – the lot!"

"Oh, Mark, this is great news!" I hug him, and we stand with our arms around each other for a while before we let go. He is staring into my eyes, with this soft dewy look. I blush furiously and look away.

"I can't wait to tell the others," I announce.

"Well, don't get too carried away. It'll take time for all the legalities to go through, and more time for all the renovation work. But months from now ..."

I am thrilled and overjoyed. At last we'll have a proper riding school and the ponies will be saved. But things get even better. When Mark and I get back home, there's a letter for me in the mailbox. It's from Carly Bridges.

"She says that Socrates is glad to be home, and she's grateful that we looked after him so well," I say, reading it to him. "And she sends us a check, to say thank you."

"That's thoughtful," says Mark. "How much?"

My eyes widen as I read the number of digits. "Well, a lot, actually," I reply, waving the check at him.

"Wow, she's generous," agrees Mark. "What are you going to do with all that money?"

"It isn't just up to me. It belongs to all of us – Ronnie, Spike and Gina," I point out. "We all took care of Socrates."

After Mark has left, I run all the way to the stables in the burning heat to tell the others. At first, Gina thinks I'm joking.

"It is hard to believe," I agree. "But it really is true."

"And let's face it, we do deserve the money," says Spike, grinning broadly.

"So, how should we spend it?" asks Ronnie. "I know what I'd like to do, if it was up to me."

"Same here," adds Gina.

"OK, you go first, Matty, since you brought us the news," suggests Spike.

"Well," I begin slowly. "I think it would be great if we spent the money on –"

"A pony!" The shouts are so unified it's hard to know who speaks first.

Of course, there are other things to consider. We have to wait until the fort is converted, so we have somewhere to keep our pony. We have to check that our parents agree (except Gina). We have to make sure that we'll have enough money to look after our pony. (We all agree to make very determined efforts to earn money.) And we have to decide what kind of pony we all want. (This last one isn't as easy as it sounds!)

Suffice to say that our parents all support the idea, as long as we promise to be responsible owners, (which we do) and we agree that our pony should be kind, "bombproof," at least six years old (we agree that a youngster would not be sensible and our parents are keen that we buy a "safe" pony), around 14 hands high to allow for us to grow (though I'm sure that I've done all my growing), and a hardy type that can live outdoors, to save on "Running Costs," as Ronnie puts it. We also agree to go to the County Horse Sale, since there are few private sellers in this area and we're likely to pay less there for our chosen purchase, enabling us to put money aside for tack and other essential equipment.

You may not be surprised to hear that I privately consider the idea of trying to buy Snowstorm from her new owners, but Mark gently points out that, even with the money that Carly Bridges has given us, Snowstorm unfortunately would still be out of our price range. I know I have to put her out of my mind once and for all, but somehow I just can't let go of this dream pony.

Well, it's very hard to be so patient when what you really want to do is rush out and buy immediately, but we know that we have to wait until the stables at the fort are ready before we can buy our pony. Still, the pot of gold at the end of the rainbow is certainly worth waiting for... And, as Ronnie rightly points out, while our lovely check sits in the bank it's earning interest!

In the meantime, life goes on, and the summer is soon over and the school term restarted by the time The Old Fort Riding Center is ready. It'll be interesting to see how it develops, but we're all full of pride and enthusiasm, convinced that it will be the best riding school in the world. Thanks to Mark, his Dad agrees to let us move our pony in before the official opening, which reduces our waiting time a little. The evening before the Horse Sales, I'm walking to the old fort with Mark, hand-in-hand (Yes, we are still getting along extremely well, thank you) to carry out a last minute inspection of the stall the girls and I prepared earlier in the day for Our New Pony.

"Don't you miss riding, just a little bit?" I ask Mark. I couldn't imagine life without riding and ponies.

He shakes his head. "Not really. I suppose it might be nice to ride now and then, just for fun, when I know I don't have to prove anything by it," he replies thoughtfully. "But at least now I get a lot more time to practice the clarinet. I'm even considering going to Music College when I graduate."

"That's good," I say, wondering if Mark and I will still be together then, and, if so, how his being away at college will affect our friendship. Still, that's a long way off...

It's starting to get dark, and tiny shafts of moonlight are casting an eerie, but romantic light over the outline of the old fort. For a while we just stand quietly gazing at the sight, and I recall the night that

Moonlight went missing and I was left alone to search for him.

"Mark, do you think that the fort is haunted?" I ask suddenly.

He looks at me, amused. "Of course not. What makes you think that? Oh, I suppose all that stuff about the ghost of the Mad Major and his spectral steed." And then, to my surprise, he starts to laugh.

"What's so funny?" I demand to know. "It's a creepy story, in my opinion."

"Yes, I suppose it is, if you fall for it."

"Fall for it?"

"Spike didn't tell you?"

"Tell me what?" I'm starting to get the feeling that I'm missing something.

"That she made it all up. She has a good sense of humor, your friend Spike."

"I know," I reply, making a mental note that Spike will be on mucking-out duty with Our New Pony for the next six months...

The following morning, Spike, Gina, Ronnie and I set off for the County Horse Sales on the bus, full of anticipation. Mark and his father have kindly agreed to

126

meet us at the sale after lunch with their horse trailer to bring back our pony, since it's too far to walk.

We have circled three possible ponies in the catalogue, but we're clearly still naive about prices, and all sell well above what we can afford, so instead we return with Comfort, an eight year old, 14.2hh bay mare who is described in the catalogue as "sweet, placid and 100% in every way." We are ecstatic. Finally, we have our own pony.

Of course, as I have learned by now, things aren't always what they seem, and in fact, Comfort turns out to be anything but a placid, problem-free pony. But, as they say, that's another story...